THE SHIELD ROAD

THE
SHIELD
ROAD

DEWI HARGREAVES

The Shield Road: A Collection of Fantasy Short Stories

Cover art and map illustration by Dewi Hargreaves; title page illustration by Rue Sparks.

This edition published in 2021

ISBN: 9798714074462

*For everyone walking
the shield road.*

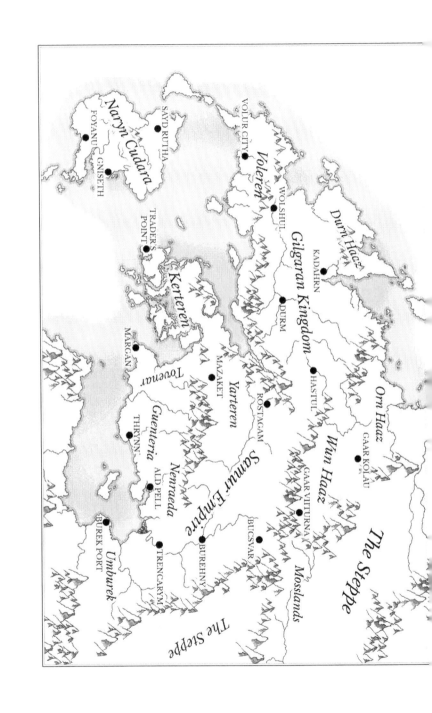

CONTENTS

PREFACE

The Shield Road is an unusual collection of short stories: the tales all take place in the same world, chronologically – one after the other. Characters, objects and themes which appear in early stories emerge again later on, and the collection follows an overarching plot that is threaded through the whole book. For these reasons, I recommend reading the stories in the order they are told.

In the year we were all shut in, the year we all experienced loss and hardship, I found great joy in following these characters on their adventures as they explored the length and breadth of the world; with us all facing months of being trapped alone, I wanted to write a collection about travel, movement, discovery – and found friendships. I hope their tales entertain you as much as they did me.

D,
At home, January 2021

THE TREE OF MORH

The horse whinnied and stamped his hooves. Rensa stroked his mane. 'Come on, Boc. Not far now.' Light wisps of snow fell on her shoulders as she waited for him to calm down. The sun was setting, and Boc hated the dark – even a horse knew it was bad to be outside during winter. The cold was dangerous, of course, but other things lurked in the frosty night in places like this.

She glanced around at the spindly trees. No movement. 'Let's go. Come on.'

Snow had been falling all day, so the road was barely visible. She led Boc by the reins, not wanting to ride him in case he panicked again. The cold seeped through her metal boots, clutching her toes. She'd left home in the dying days of summer, but winter came fast to the north – and lingered far longer.

All this for a potion. She could laugh. How many adventures had she been on? How much treasure had she found? And now she was risking it all for the sake of a bottle.

But that bottle meant everything to her.

Darkness fell as the sun dropped behind the hills. Boc whinnied. They carried on, one foot in front of the other. Rensa focused on the rhythmic clinking of her chainmail and the wind blowing through the branches.

They climbed a steep hill. When they reached the top, Rensa grinned and patted Boc's side. There, at the bottom of the valley, was the cabin. A single candle danced in the window and cast a glow over the frost.

Hopefully she'd have what Rensa needed.

Rensa looped Boc's reins around a post and passed through the open gate.

Before she could knock, a voice called from inside. 'Come in.'

She opened the old door. The room was cramped and dimly lit, the soft light coming from the candle and a dying fire. Shelves covered every inch of the walls, crammed full of jars and bottles and small boxes covered in dust.

There was a single chair beside the fire. It wasn't large, but it dwarfed the skinny woman who sat in it. Her straight, white hair fell around her shoulders. A scar cut across her right cheek from the corner of her mouth. Her skin was ashen.

'I wondered if you'd make it before nightfall, or if I'd have to go out and find you.'

Rensa blinked. 'How did you know I was coming?'

The witch laughed. 'I see everyone who comes to my cabin.' She pushed herself up. 'Now let's go and see to your horse.'

Rensa scowled. 'I suppose you know why I'm here as well,' she said as they went outside.

'I have a vague idea,' the witch said. 'But I want to hear you say it.'

Rensa's face flushed, which angered her. This was nothing to be embarrassed about. She'd faced far worse in her life.

But love was always terrifying.

'I want you to help me make a potion.'

She took Boc's reins and followed the witch behind the cabin to a rickety wooden stable. It looked as though it hadn't been used in years.

'Oh, I know thousands of potions,' the witch said. 'But you want a particular type of potion, don't you?'

'You already know what it is.'

She shut the stable door and found the witch smirking at her. 'I want to hear you say it.'

She looked away. 'I need a love potion.'

***

Theod shuddered despite the cloak wrapped around him.

'Too far,' he muttered to himself. 'Much too far.'

But when the cabin came into view, he didn't regret his journey.

To his surprise, the door was already open. He doused his lantern and moved off the track, watching from the safety of a bush. *Has she been attacked?* It was possible. The nights were drawing in, and when winter hit the north, all kinds of creatures emerged from their dark holes – some much worse than others.

The witch emerged from behind the cabin, closely followed by a tall woman in chainmail. The witch's laugh echoed up the valley.

What was this? He'd been told the witch lived alone.

He forced his insecurity down. They didn't look like bad types. Besides, he had nowhere else to go. If he slept out in the woods, he'd freeze to death.

He waited until they'd gone inside. Then, steeling his nerves, he prepared to knock on the door.

Voices inside stopped him.

'…don't do memory magic. It's too powerful, too easy to abuse. Only a few are trusted to use it, and even they have proven treacherous sometimes.'

There was silence.

'Hello, Theod,' came the witch's voice.

He paused, hand on the door. She knew his name.

He entered slowly, meeting the eyes of the warrior; dark brown and, right now, full of suspicion, if not outright hostility. Her black hair was knotted up tightly on top of her head and her dark skin was rough, hardened by a life on the road.

'Who is he?' she said.

When Theod didn't speak, the witch answered. 'Theod. He's here for the same reason you are, Rensa.'

'I – I don't think so,' Theod said. 'I'm not here for war potions. My needs have nothing to do with fighting at all.'

'Nor do mine,' the warrior snapped.

Theod looked at the ground.

'Isn't this interesting?' the witch said, clapping her hands. 'No-one's come to me for a love potion in years, then two arrive on the very same day. Unfortunately, I can't make them anymore. I don't have the ingredients.'

He cursed himself. He knew this trip was folly. What a fool he'd been, and not for the first time.

'What, you mean amongst all this,' Rensa said, gesturing at the shelves, 'you don't have the things to make a love potion?'

'Well, people stopped asking for them!' the witch replied. 'But it's a simple recipe. I can use substitutes. Only one ingredient is truly essential: the leaves of a morh tree.'

'I've never heard of it,' Theod said.

'Neither have I,' Rensa said.

'I'm not surprised. They're not very common these days.' Rensa rolled her eyes. 'Where do I find this tree?'

'There's one north of here. Follow the stream up, you'll see it. The other trees have dropped their leaves, but the morh grows all year. I need two leaves.' The witch smiled, holding up two scrawny fingers. 'You must work together.'

'I don't think so,' Rensa said sharply. 'I'll be quicker on my own.'

'Trust me, it takes two to take a morh's leaves,' the witch said, then wagged her finger. 'And don't you go pulling at it, either. It will only give you its leaves if it wants to. Else they won't grow back – and it'd probably kill you, anyway.'

Theod wished he'd never come at all.

'And that's all we need?' Rensa asked.

'That's all you need,' the witch said with a smile, before producing a small bottle. 'But if you could just fill this with water from the stream, too, that would be wonderful. Take the water from beside the morh. Not further down or higher up – I'll know.'

***

Next morning, Theod's muscles ached.

The air was colder than it had been the night before. This miserable, frigid bedroom was nothing like home. He missed his carpets, his roaring hearth, and the warm breakfast that usually awaited him. As it was, he chewed a piece of bread, threw his cloak on, and fell out the cabin door, trying not to think about the day ahead.

Rensa set off without looking at him. 'Come on then, don't dawdle.'

He resisted the urge to snap back. If they were going to spend the day together, it was best not to start a fight.

Now it was light, he could truly see the place he'd found himself in. There was a harsh beauty to it. In summer it would be gorgeous: glistening lakes nestled between craggy ridges, the sunlight kissing the heathland. In winter it was a different place, though. Fog rolled down the hills, and the branches of dead trees reached through it like clumps of fingers. He walked with his head down, watching the ground and leaving Rensa far behind. More than once, his feet threatened to give way on the steep slopes.

Then they did.

He rolled through the snow, gaining speed, before slamming into something.

It was Rensa.

She stared at him. *Is that the hint of a smirk?*

'Not used to this, hm?'

She pulled him to his feet with one hand.

'And I suppose you've spent years traipsing through the snow?' he asked, dusting off his cloak.

'You'd be surprised.'

'Must be pretty old, then,' he said, and saw a flash of anger in her eyes. He swiftly changed the subject. 'Why are you here? Surely a warrior has more important things to do than go around bothering witches?'

She looked away, studying the horizon. The question hung in the air, but he didn't let it go.

'If we're doing this, I need to know why you're here at least,' he said.

'I want a partner.'

He stifled his laugh. 'You mean a husband? That's a strange career move.'

'Not a husband,' she growled. 'I mean a partner. Someone who'll keep me company, adventure with me. You Guenterians and your husbands and wives.'

'There's nothing wrong with being wedded,' he said. 'They'd stay your partner for life then. And your union would be blessed by the Four.'

She grimaced. 'We don't do that where I'm from. Besides, all relationships are blessed by the Four. Don't need some vows and a bit of paper for that; it's in the heart.'

Theod studied her face. Short, bunched-up hair, pinched wrinkles appearing around her eyes, a hard nose. She was the very portrait of a warrior, but beneath that was a softness that he'd missed the first time he saw her.

'I'm not as fast as I was,' she continued. 'Need someone to watch my back. That's all.'

'And a little fun on the side?'

She didn't reply, but there was the phantom of a smile on her lips.

They found the stream and followed it into the hills. Snow crunched beneath his feet. No birds chirped and for a while, no wind blew, though snow continued to float down. He watched the snowflakes melt in Rensa's hair as she marched.

'What about you?' she asked.

'Me?'

'Why do you need the potion?'

He was reluctant to give an answer. But she'd offered him one, so it was only fair. 'There's a girl in my town…'

'Ah,' she said. 'And she doesn't like you enough on her own? Needs some convincing?'

'Maybe,' he said after a while.

'And you're comfortable with that?'

'At least I won't get her killed,' he snapped. 'You're tricking someone into a suicide pact.'

Rensa's face twisted, but she held her words. 'It's not a trick,' she eventually muttered.

'It is. Face it, we're both tricksters.'

***

'There!' Rensa said.

The sun had passed the middle of the sky. At the top of a snowy ridge, surrounded by black trees, was a tree with gold-brown bark, a trunk supporting a perfect sphere of blue leaves.

It had taken long enough. The sun had passed the middle of the sky, and Rensa's calves ached from the ascent.

'Do you think that's it?' Theod asked.

'What else would it be?'

He blushed. She looked him over, this small man dwarfed by his cloak and expensive furs. His clear complexion betrayed his noble heritage, while his copper skin and preoccupation with marriage marked him as a Guenterian. Out here in the wilds it was painfully obvious he'd lived a life of luxury, with his short, neat hair and thin beard. It surprised her he'd even made it this far. But there was a determination in his eyes that cut through the delicateness and demanded respect. And the blade at his hip – its scabbard was not new. It had seen use.

She paused at the base of the morh. Pressing her hand to the bark, she found it almost warm.

'Morh, can we please have two of your precious leaves?'

The branches shuddered in the wind. Nothing.

Theod sniggered.

She glared at him. 'Any better ideas?'

'No,' he said, shrugging. 'Would have been nice if the witch gave us a hint.'

Rensa looked up. The leaves were too high for a single person to grab. 'She said it would take two of us. What if I lifted you up? You'd be able to reach.'

'She told us not to pull on them,' Theod said. 'Besides, I doubt it's going to be that simple.' He wiped the snow off a fallen log and sat on it. He was panting.

'Not used to all this physical activity?' she said with half a smile.

'My endurance is good,' he complained. 'I could *walk* for miles. Climbing is another thing.'

'Of course.'

She circled the tree. Perhaps there was a hollow with something inside? Or at least a place to leave an offering? Though that wouldn't explain why it needed two of them. Not unless it wanted a human sacrifice. But that seemed unlikely for a tree of love.

The bark was smooth and flaky. She was almost afraid to touch it. By the gods, she'd been everywhere, from the frozen isles of the far north to the hot, red mountains of the east. She knew every magical plant and savage monster there was, but she'd never once heard of a morh tree. Unless the tree was known by another name elsewhere.

Even then, she'd never seen a tree with blue leaves.

'Come and help,' she said, but turned around to find Theod's eyes closed. 'What are you doing?'

'Thinking,' he replied. 'And resting.'

'Looks a lot more like resting than thinking.'

'That's the thing about thinking,' he said without opening his eyes. 'You can't see it.'

Insufferable. What a waste of time to send them both out here. He was useless.

Another loop around the tree revealed nothing. She was tempted to draw her axe and cut it down in frustration.

She took a deep breath. *Time for a walk.* Theod could freeze for all she cared.

Finding herself back at the stream, she sat on a rock and watched the water trickle over the pebbles. She pulled out the bottle the witch had given her and held it in the water, corking it once it was full.

The tree loomed on the ridge, its shadow growing longer as the sun drifted towards the horizon. They would have to head back soon. And while she'd seen no sign of anything unusual on their journey north, winter was close.

The wraiths would be out any night now.

It was the right choice to leave Boc in the stable.

She drew her axe and traced the blade with her finger. *Damn that tree. And damn that witch for not being any clearer.* How long were they expected to keep this up? Would they have to spend another day hiking all the way up here, only to find no answers?

A flicker of movement caught her attention. The bushes rustled behind her. A black figure rushed across the snow - too fast to be human.

A curdling screech pierced the air, scattering the birds.

She was on her feet in a second, axe raised. Theod stumbled down the ridge, sword drawn. Another figure hurtled towards him.

Rensa fell.

***

Her body was cold. Covered in snow. No feeling in her arms.
She knew what that meant.

Blinking, she saw Theod standing over her. Inky darkness
surrounded them, but somewhere he'd found a torch. How
long had they been there? Her body trembled.

Sword in hand, he was waving the fire at something. A
half-formed shape in the darkness, a darker shadow with
sharp eyes and a jagged mouth. Her stomach dropped.

***

His arm was numb where the shadow wraith touched him,
but his half-dead fingers still gripped the torch tight: he
knew if he dropped it, it was over.

He shoved the fire into the shade's face and it screamed
as it burned. Lashing out with his sword, he cut it down. It
collapsed onto the snow, a shredded pile of ribbons.

Rensa was shivering violently, her pupils pale and
unseeing. He was no expert, but he knew what the touch of
a wraith could do. It was as though the cold was within her.

Another wraith came wailing out of the darkness,
swinging dark, shadowed claws. Sweeping, he caught it with
the torch and brought his sword around, slicing through it.
Others circled like birds of prey just outside the torch's glow.

'Stay back!'

He sounded so weak.

The wind blew hard, making the morh's branches rattle
like bones. The flames quivered, but the wraiths didn't come
any closer. His sword glinted in the torchlight, its surface
coated in the rainbow sheen of oil.

They understood.

Turning his attention to Rensa, he cut his cloak in half
and placed one strip on the snow. Slowly, agonisingly, he

rolled her onto it with one hand. He wrapped her in the other half and lay next to her, using the torch's meagre heat for warmth.

They stayed like that for what felt like eternity, watching the wraiths' hungry eyes and open maws gawping from the dark. But Rensa's trembles slowly eased. She finally closed her eyes, her breathing steadying.

Two blue leaves fell, landing on the snow beside his face.

***

When she woke, there was an awful numbness in her shoulders. Whole patches of her arms and torso still lacked feeling. Her legs felt heavy.

The room was small but warm. She'd been here before, but couldn't remember when.

'Good morning,' said a man sitting on the bottom of her bed. Theod, his dark hair matted and his cheeks pale. There were bags under his eyes.

When he smiled, she remembered it all.

She pushed herself up.

'You should've run away,' she said.

'Yeah, I should've.'

'Fool,' she said – but found herself smiling. 'What happened to your cloak?'

'It's a long story.'

'What about the tree? Did you get the leaves?'

He nodded.

She slumped back down, exhausted. A laugh escaped her lips. 'There's more to you than I first thought.'

'I wasn't going to die over a silly blue tree.' He grinned.

'The wraiths. How did you…?'

He drew a bottle and rag from his pocket and the room filled with the sharp, metallic stench of the magic oil.

A monster-hunter's weapon. 'You are a mystery.'

'I'm not that complicated, really,' he said with a smile, but he couldn't hide his exhaustion.

Over time, the numbness fell away and she was able to stand. To her surprise, the main room was deserted.

'Where's the witch?'

'She left. Made a potion in a little green bottle. She was frowning a lot. Said she had business to attend to in the south, and she didn't fancy staying here now the wraiths are out. Said we should get going too. But she left your potion.'

'Potion? Just one?'

With that he pulled out a red, corked bottle and gave it to her. His cheeks flushed, and he couldn't meet her eye.

'I don't need one anymore.'

TOMB

The witch followed an old road that cut through the white highlands like a scar. It was bare earth, though ancient cobbles poked through here and there.

This would be a harsh winter, she could tell already. She hoped Rensa would recover quickly.

Beside the road lay a glittering lake, crystal blue in the harsh northern sunlight. Its surface was smooth like glass; the water barely rippled on its rocky banks.

She took a deep breath and dived in.

The cold seeped into her bones, but she swam down, down, until the light was almost gone.

Embedded in the silt were two old, tall rocks, covered in swirling marks. Between them lay a stone door, its two halves sealed. A face was etched into it, a face with tired eyes, a bulbous nose, and a long beard like a waterfall, tickled by tiny green plants that swayed as she approached.

She touched the door and the stones parted.

The water remained where it was. She stepped out, falling to her knees as she adjusted to the weight of her wet, heavy clothes. The door closed behind her, plunging her into total darkness.

She felt around in her pouch and pulled out a gemstone roughly the size of her hand: a moongem. Its dull blue glow pulsed, bouncing off the icy roof of the tunnel she found herself in.

She walked. Small pebbles dotted the floor, and a tiny hole to her left went down forever and smelled faintly of sulphur.

The tunnel curved right and opened into a large cavern. A narrow walkway crossed a pool in the middle. Three pillars stood either side of it, jutting out of the water. Each was a stack of stone heads with thick beards and big noses, turned green by moss and lichen.

She crossed the cavern, her footsteps echoing off the high roof, and entered a corridor which led to a large, square room. Ancient runes covered the walls.

In the centre of the room was a raised dais on which a glacial boulder rested. Balanced on the boulder was a solitary helmet, its eyeholes dark. There was not a spot of rust on it.

At the base of the boulder lay a stone bowl which cradled a wreath of twelve fresh flowers. She bent down to inspect them. Red, orange, yellow and white. They still held their fresh scents, as though they were picked yesterday.

'I know you're here,' she whispered.

A grey-skinned man stepped out of the dark. Swirling tattoos covered his arms, some of them runes in a language long forgotten by many.

But not her.

'What brings you, witch?'

'A suspicion.'

The grey man watched her carefully from the corner, but didn't move.

He nodded.

She stepped forward, laying her hands on the helm.

She saw a vision. A vision of fire, of black anger, of charred wood and bones and the wreckage of a city framed by a dying red sun, piercing screams filling the twilight air.

She saw the thoughts of a Keeper, and they disturbed her greatly.

THE THIEF

'Are we agreed?' she said.

'Not so fast.' Hovil turned the box over in his hands, studying it. He glanced up at her. He had dark eyes, shadowed and suspicious. The eyes of a manipulator. Someone who could draw brutal deals out of the most desperate people.

He opened the box and peered inside, then rubbed the object with his finger as though removing dirt.

'I don't recognise this sigil. Where did you get this?'

Her throat almost closed.

'I found it.'

'Of course.' Placing the box on the counter, he leaned forward and stared. 'And this person you found it from, are they likely to go looking for it?'

'No.' She struggled to keep her voice level. 'They're dead.'

'How?'

'Accident.'

'Were you involved?'

'No. It was long ago.'

'I see.' His face betrayed nothing. Reaching under the desk, he fiddled with some papers, then dug out a pen. Her heart pounded as the nib scratched away.

He reached into his pouch. 'Then you can have your ten silvers.'

Relief swamped her. 'Excellent.'

His smug smile told her everything. He was a swindler. And this, he was thinking, was his best catch of the month.

She didn't care. If all he'd offered was a single copper, she'd have taken it.

She just wanted it gone.

She snatched the coins and thanked him courteously, but he was already eyeing up another prize.

His gaze followed the curves of her body. 'Is that a Nenraedan tunic?'

She left without another word.

As she hurried down the street, she heard a skittering on the roof tiles above. Looking up, she caught sight of the corner of someone's cloak.

She cursed.

***

Burse slammed her hand on the table, making the inn's patrons wince. 'You'd better find the money from somewhere, you cretin, or I'll throw you out in the street.'

Rafi refused to meet her eye. She was a giant of a person, wide and tall. Having made her money smuggling, she'd settled down to run a sailor's inn – and run herself into an early grave, judging by how much she drank.

A native of Voleren, she stood out amongst her patrons because of her pale skin. Nearly everyone else in the room, Rafi included, was a copper-skinned Guenterian.

She was also prone to fits of temper. When that happened, Rafi knew it was best to keep his head down.

It wasn't like he was paying for much. A tiny room in the attic and the right to sit in the common room after hours. Hardly luxurious, especially for four silvers a fortnight.

Nowhere else would take him in, though. Even in a city as large as Thrynn, there were precious few innkeeps who'd house a thief. Burse knew it too.

'I'll find it,' Rafi told her.

She leered. 'You will. Or you'll be living in the gutter. Least 'til a warden throws you in the harbour.'

Might be better than having old crones like you howl at me all day, he wanted to say. He held his tongue, but a smirk spread across his face.

'It's funny?'

There was a sharpened edge to those words. He shook his head.

She glared. 'Two days. I want the coins in two days, or you're gone. Unless you're willing to give up that blade-'

'Never.'

'Then find the coin.'

He watched her stalk away and dreamt of putting the blade between her ears. He pulled it from its sheath, the lithe dagger with a red pommel. On it was printed the shield-shaped badge of the University of Rostagam, a reminder of happier times.

Two days to find four silvers? An artisan would struggle to earn that, let alone a vagabond like himself.

But he was already on his feet. Because he had a craft of his own, and he plied it at night.

***

Rafi watched the warden march past from the shelter of a dark alley. The lantern-light drifted down the road, leaving him in total darkness.

But Rafi knew where he was going.

These streets were like home to him: he knew them back to front. He scurried like a rat, ducking the night wardens and flitting from shadow to shadow. It wasn't difficult. Most of them were elderly. They followed their patrol routes with time-worn instinct, hardly bothering to look for trouble.

Crime was easy in Thrynn.

He made his way to the market square. Here, the prospective thief could find the best pickings – and the toughest challenges.

Avoiding the main road, he dodged down a muddy backstreet where the buildings were cramped and tilted. Behind a vacant shop was a cart, piled high with sealed barrels. They'd sat there for years. He did not know what was in them, nor did he care – but they were an efficient route to the rooftops.

He walked cautiously over the roof tiles and took a seat. From up here, the entire square was visible. In the centre were the market stalls, most of which had been dismantled and covered with cloth to protect them from the dew. Two wardens stood talking beside a burning brazier. One wobbled and had to clutch the other's shoulder; they were clearly deep in their drink. Another three plodded around the edge of the square, shining their lanterns through windows occasionally as they passed the storefronts.

Most of the stores were artisans' workshops. They were easy pickings, but there wasn't much to be found inside. Rafi's fence wasn't interested in blacksmiths' tongs or carpenters' knives. She wanted something more valuable.

His eyes came to rest on Hovil's pawnshop. Hovil was the worst kind of pawnbroker. He'd buy things for cheap when people were struggling then sell them back with huge interest. Rafi knew at least a dozen people who'd happily cut his eyes out.

He would gleefully rob such a man.

Plus, he'd seen a stranger visit his shop recently. A woman wearing an expensive red Nenraedan tunic. She'd looked nervous. Of course, many people who came to Thrynn did – usually rural folk who were unused to the city's crowds. But hers was a different kind of anxiety. The kind that was trying to hide something, and he could see that a mile away.

She thought her tunic could hide her armour, but not from him.

Her kind often had urgent need of pawnshops; looters, tomb-robbers and adventurers carrying strange items from one place to another, hoping to sell them and make enough money to fund their next expedition.

It was time to pay Hovil a visit.

Rafi clambered down and skirted through the alleys, entering the market square via a long-abandoned back passage. He twirled the lockpick restlessly between his fingers as he watched the wardens. No matter how many times he did this, it still made his heart race. Flicking his black hair out of his face, he eyed up Hovil's shop.

Like much of Thrynn, it was slowly sinking into the mud. Rot was building up around the base, blackening the wooden walls. The back half was sinking faster than the front, putting the door at an angle. But no-one ever went to a pawnshop for the décor.

When the way was clear, he sprang at the door, fumbling with the lock. Stab. Stab. *Click*. The door swung inwards with a creak and he darted through, closing it behind him.

Hovil's shop was a tangled mess. As Rafi crept over the floorboards, he dodged piles of old things – here an old iron pot, there a broken brooch. He passed bent tools and dusty bottles, pots and jugs and the occasional rolled-up rug or carpet. It reminded him of the Thrynn Library, where his friend Kazir worked. He'd broken in there twice. Unlike these things, though, the objects there had actual value. Some were centuries old and had to be preserved in glass cases.

A vague sadness tugged at him, but he shook it off. One day, he'd go back to his studies.

He was ready to give up when something caught his eye.

A small wooden box lying on the counter.

The box was small enough to fit snugly in his hand. Its rounded edges were smooth to the touch and a deep varnish gave it the texture of a horse-chestnut. He opened it.

A small silver pendant rested on a bed of black wool. It was diamond-shaped, but its face was flat. It bore a family crest – a pair of crow's wings framing the head of a fox, outlined with filigree. Two orange gems peered out from the fox's face: bright, fiery eyes.

Not a crest he recognised.

It looked expensive. The gems alone would fetch a good profit. The silver could be melted down and wrought into something else. Exactly how that happened was the fence's job, though.

He'd won his prize, and he'd get his reward.

***

Rafi couldn't sleep. His skin was hot, almost feverish, despite the winter weather. The bedding was too warm; it made him sweat. He checked the hearth in case he'd left the fire going, but it was cold.

When he finally slept, he dreamt.

First there were two orange orbs, glowing like distant lanterns. As they came closer, a body emerged. A snow fox with the wooden box in its jaws.

He tried to grab the animal, but it ran. He gave chase, sprinting down shadowed streets that looked like Thrynn, though he didn't recognise the buildings. He followed the glow of the fox's eyes, thinking of nothing else.

They came to a high stone wall with a gatehouse. The fox slipped under the portcullis and disappeared.

He looked up to see the front gate of Castle Thrynn. Some deep instinct within him told him this was his home. He eyed up the tall towers. Those banners, they were *wrong*. They weren't his. They belonged to someone else – someone he knew. A large, bearded man. Rafi couldn't remember his name, but he knew his face.

It was a snarling face. It loomed over him, grinning awfully, torch in hand. He was in bed now, the man holding him down. Coarse rope bit into his legs and shoulders. The man dropped the torch and left. The room burned.

***

Rafi awoke and found himself standing before the gate of Castle Thrynn. He was still in his bedclothes. His teeth chattered and his body shook as the frigid dawn air nipped his flesh.

Looking up, he saw nothing but the stone walls he saw every other time he passed it. The banners flying from the towers, dragged by the wind, showed Lord Bedivar's colours: a grinning white crescent moon on dark blue cloth.

Lord Bedivar. Was it his face Rafi saw in the dream? He couldn't be sure. He'd only ever seen the lord in portraits, and the dream was already slipping from memory.

'What are you doing there, scoundrel? Clear off!'

A bearded man waved a spear from the walls.

Rafi shook his head. What was he doing?

He retreated down the hill and returned to the inn, his mind restless. *It was just a bad dream*, he told himself as he dressed. Probably brought on by worry. He hadn't burgled in a while. It was playing on his mind. But once he sold the pendant to his fence, his conscience would be clear. It wouldn't be his problem anymore.

His fingers itched to hold it again.

***

He slipped into a tavern halfway down a backstreet.

'Hello Rafi,' said the soft, familiar voice.

'Hello Zenya.'

She smirked, standing behind the counter of what most would have thought was an ordinary tavern. He knew it, however, as a place to sell off unwanted – and previously owned – objects.

'I thought you'd given up the rob?' she said.

He winced. 'I needed the money fast.'

'I'm not complaining. What you got for me?'

He gripped the box. For some reason, the idea of handing it over made his stomach churn. *Madness*. Why did he feel so connected to this chunk of silver? All he wanted was the damn coin.

He pushed the feeling down and gave her the box.

'Hmm. I have to say, I've never seen anything like this. I mean, the composition is pretty standard. The silver is nothing to shout about and the stones are citrine, though well cut and a nice, deep colour. But the design…'

'How much?'

She pouted. 'Having a bad day? Alright. I'd say it's worth thirty silvers to me—'

There was a knock at the door. Rafi turned to see a warden entering. He was very young, his tawny brown face almost childlike behind his dark, wispy beard. He touched his hand to his helmet as he crossed the threshold. 'Good day. I wanted to ask you a few questions about Hovil's shop.'

Rafi's breath caught in his throat. He stepped aside to let the warden forward. Zenya side-eyed him.

'Hovil, right. Isn't that the pawnshop owner?' she said.

'It is,' the warden confirmed. 'His shop was broken into last night. He says they stole something of great personal value.'

'Oh, really?' Zenya said, with a subtle glance at Rafi. 'And why should I know anything about that?'

'I'm not saying you should. But I'm sure you won't mind if I have a quick look around?'

There was an edge to his voice.

'I suppose not,' Zenya eventually replied.

Both disappeared into the storeroom. Zenya left the box on the counter, and Rafi snatched it up. He took a seat at one of the tavern tables, figuring it best to appear casual and not arouse suspicion. He fought to keep his breathing calm. His hand remained clasped around the box in his pocket.

They returned. 'Well, you've got odd things back there for a tavern, but nothing that matches our description.'

'Please bring a warrant next time,' Zenya said. 'I'm not always in the mood to let people go poking around in my private areas.'

The warden left quickly.

Once she was sure he was gone, Zenya fixed Rafi with a glare. 'Did you get that necklace from Hovil?'

'No,' he said, too slowly.

'Rafi…'

He scowled. 'So you don't want it now?'

'I'm not as interested as I was a few minutes ago,' she said. 'Look. Come by next week, when the wardens have given up the chase. We'll work something out. But only because I like you.'

'I don't have a week.'

'You'll wait a week, or you'll get nothing,' she said with a shrug. 'Nothing personal. It's just business.'

***

That night, it snowed in Thrynn.

Rafi watched the flakes drift over the city. His bedroom was too hot. After lying down for a few moments, sweat would stream down his face and he'd have to find some water. Where would he wake up tomorrow? Outside the castle again? Or somewhere worse?

He sat on his bed, cradling the pendant in his hands and staring into its orange eyes. It was rare that he ever felt a connection to anything; he'd never have called himself sentimental. How much jewellery had he happily stolen and sold in the past? In all that time, he'd never had a second thought. This? This was different.

A noise disturbed his thoughts.

Click click. It came from the window. A bird pecking the glass?

Click click. Slowly, he crossed the room, heart pounding in his ears. He opened the curtain.

Nothing.

From his room at the top of the inn, he could see a big swathe of the city. All was black. Except…

A dull glow. A pair of licking flames inside the castle gatehouse.

Frozen to the spot, he watched as the flames engulfed the castle with astonishing speed. Soon the entire building was ablaze. His eyes were drawn to the window of a tower. In that window, he swore he saw a silhouette.

The pendant rattled in its box. When he opened it, the fox's eyes glowed like the core of a bonfire.

He woke drenched in sweat, lying on the floorboards of his tiny room. Sunlight streamed in through the window. The pendant was on the floor.

He scrambled to his feet and looked outside. To his surprise, the castle was untouched. A couple of figures patrolled the walls in their usual slow, lazy way. Nothing had changed.

He scooped up the pendant and shut it away in the box. His legs were shuddering. This was too much for him to handle alone.

But he knew who to speak to.

***

The Library was one of the oldest buildings in Thrynn – or so his friend Kazir said. It was a towering stone structure, with tall windows that couldn't be reached from the ground. Kazir told him this was so the light came in from higher up, making it easier for him and the other scholars to read and write, but Rafi suspected it was more to keep people like himself out.

Not that it worked.

He took his usual route, climbing onto a low-cut roof and treading carefully across the fresh snow on the tiles. From there he leapt onto a ledge he knew led straight to Kazir's study.

Sure enough, his old friend was in there, wearing his emerald robe, hunched over a book. His grey hair was thinning, his round face red. Rafi knocked on the glass.

Kazir used a pole to wind the window open and Rafi dropped down.

'What in the world are you doing?' Kazir hissed, pushing up his spectacles. 'I'm in the middle of something.'

'Long time no see,' Rafi said.

He scowled. 'I don't have time for games. I'll find you in the tavern after hours.'

'Kazir, please, this is important.'

The scribe sighed. 'You're going to get me in trouble one day. What is it?'

'I have a question.'

'And there was no-one else in the entire city who could answer your question?'

'It's a history question,' Rafi said with a smile.

'Ah.' Kazir straightened. 'Well, go ahead.'

He hesitated. 'Has the castle ever burned down before?'

Kazir rubbed his chin. 'Hmm. No. But there was a fire in one of the towers a century ago. It was a big event, but people forget history too quickly.'

Rafi ignored his complaining. 'Did anyone die in the fire?'

Kazir pursed his lips and frowned. He paced across the room. 'They did.' He wagged a finger. 'I have a feeling you know more than you're letting on.'

Rafi remembered the dream and shivered. 'I know a little. Who was it?'

'Lord Lovican. A wicked man, by almost anyone's telling. I won't discuss those rumours, that's not my place, but some supposedly awful things happened behind those walls while he was there. His court worked to cover most of it up.'

His stomach turned over. 'A wicked man?'

Kazir grimaced. 'A wicked man, and long-lived. The people feared he'd be in power forever.'

'How did the fire happen?'

Kazir tugged his collar. 'Nobody knows. A fire started in Lord Lovican's tower – who knows what he was doing in there – and he wasn't able to escape in time. Lovican left no heirs. The castle, the city and the whole Woldland thus fell into the hands of the Bedivar family, who rule benevolently to this day.' He pointed at Rafi. 'And pay for my livelihood, so don't you go accusing them of anything.'

A wave of irrational hatred hit him at the mention of their name. He'd never so much as given the Bedivars a second thought before. Why did he care so much now?

'Lovican's entire lineage is a mystery,' Kazir was saying. 'We know his crest, though.'

Icy dread tickled Rafi's spine. 'Did it look like this?' He pulled out the pendant.

Kazir peered over his spectacles. 'Why, yes. By the Four, where did you find that?'

'I might have found it. In Hovil's shop.'

Kazir flinched. 'So it was you. I should've known. The wardens have been all over the city for that damned thing.' He shook his head. 'You're never going to learn, are you?'

'I've learned about Lord Lovican,' Rafi said. 'And I've learned that I want nothing to do with this damned necklace.' He heard the weariness in his own voice. 'But it is strangely alluring. It's hard to give away.'

Kazir smiled. It was not a nice smile. 'You know, they say Lovican had an unusual power over people. They always wanted to be near him. He was awful, of course – his bride ran out after three days, screaming, and was never seen again. But women and men alike were always drawn to him, as though he had some kind of power over them. They trusted him.'

***

Rafi couldn't sleep.

It was as though Kazir's story had stirred something. A deep rage burned through him, coursing in his blood. He hated the castle, he hated the city, he hated that grinning moon banner.

It all had to burn.

He sat up in a panic when he realised those words weren't his own. They were the thoughts of someone else.

Throwing the curtains open, he leaned out the window for some fresh air. A flock of crows scattered, cawing angrily.

There was a light in Castle Thrynn. In the high window of the tower, a silhouette stared back.

'*Burn. Burn. Burn.*'

***

It was a white, misty morning when Osirit pushed his key in the lock. He saw a crow glide overhead and perch on the tiled roof across the street, watching him closely. There was a fiery glint in its eyes, a glint that pulled him out of his usual morning thoughts and set him on edge.

Many called him superstitious, but he didn't like crows at the best of times, and this one was up to no good.

The familiar musty scent of his shop hit him as he entered and looked around. Everything was as he'd left it yesterday.

That wasn't something he usually worried about, but since Hovil's shop the other side of the city was broken into twice, he'd been incredibly cautious.

His boots clunked on the bare floorboards as he crossed the room and fell into his old armchair. He picked up a small wooden duck from the table and took out his whittling knife, continuing from where he'd stopped the night before. His thoughts drifted back to Hovil. Poor man. If the rumours were true, he lost something of great value that night. And why someone would break in just to burn the place, a day after it was robbed, made no sense to Osirit at all.

The door opened, startling him.

'Good morning,' he said, jumping to his feet and running a hand through his unruly red hair. *A bit early for a customer.*

A young man entered, eyes firmly on the ground. His cheeks were drawn, his black hair unkempt. It was the face of a man touched by poverty, an expression Osirit was all too used to seeing.

'Morning,' the man mumbled. He opened his hand. On his palm sat a smooth wooden box.

Osirit took it and examined it carefully. Exquisitely made. He popped the latch open and stared into the bejewelled eyes of a silver fox. A talented pair of hands had made this, an experienced and confident jeweller at the height of their skill.

Looking at the man in front of him, he knew it had to be stolen. People like him didn't come by things like this any other way.

But that was none of his business. He knew he'd find a buyer for it faster than anyone could track it.

'Beautiful, beautiful,' Osirit murmured. 'Wonderfully made. Of course I'll take it. Fifteen silvers seems fair to me. Family heirloom?' he asked, raising his eyebrows.

'Something like that.'

THE SILENT STONES

Nerena approached the stones that were always silent. Her earliest memory was of asking her father where they'd come from. His answer?

'They've always been here, little one.'

They weren't far from the village.

Their village lay in a secluded valley at the bottom of the mountains, a cluster of round huts with white walls and dark roofs. There was a lumber mill on the far side, powered by the mountain stream that came loud and fast from the slopes above. It had been years since the Empire's agents last visited, to perform what they called a 'Sensuss of Forriners.' They swept through on fresh white horses, carrying red and gold banners and saying something about the right of conquest. No-one paid them much mind. They'd been doing so for decades, and the villagers had quickly learned just to nod at whatever they said and give them food. They always left soon enough.

A dusty path ran from the village into the mountains. The shepherds used it because they liked to pasture their animals on the open green at the top, between the old ruins that stretched into the sky. At night, the children would go up there and tell tales of ghosts.

The silent stones lay beside that path.

There was something strange about them. Three stacks of rough rocks piled up to head height, a triangular boulder sitting on top. That was the best way to describe them. Three perfectly smooth sides forming a sharp point, it was as though the stacks were three fingers holding an arrowhead pointing to the heavens. She called them the silent stones because she heard no noise near them, not even the rustle of leaves or the calls of birds.

An eerie silent patch on the otherwise normal ascent from the village. The dark stones always seemed to leave an imprint on her mind long after she'd passed them.

Nerena walked by them less in adulthood, since there was little reason to make the climb. She no longer told ghost stories, after all, and she was no shepherd.

But she walked by them now. And as she did, she heard a noise.

Ducking into the grass, she saw a flickering light. A single candle standing on the ground beside the stones.

As she watched, a figure emerged from the trees. A man, thin and malnourished, with hair down to his shoulders. His face was noble and kind, with bright eyes and a firm mouth. He knelt before the candle and placed his hands delicately in his lap, which was covered by a simple shawl that left his arms visible. They were covered in faded, snaking tattoos tangled around ancient runes. He bowed his head.

It was not a man she recognised. She knew every man in the village, and their village was as far from the main road as it was possible to be. Not even the lost travellers made it as far as their valley.

Which meant he was here for a reason.

She studied him for a long time, wondering what connection he had to her childhood stones. *Could he have built them?* She doubted it. It would have been impossible alone, and besides, he had no muscle to speak of. But he looked unnervingly like he was from the village.

The only other folks they saw were Empire folks from Sameren, and they were golden, soft-skinned. He looked as though he could have been a brother or cousin of hers. His facial features were familiar, though his skin was stone grey.

'Hello,' she said.

The man looked up as though he'd heard an arrow flying towards him.

'Who are you?' she asked.

His eyes locked on hers. Grey eyes, kind and gentle – and full of terror.

Still no reply, so she tried again. 'What are you doing here? Have you been here before?'

He jumped to his feet, glancing around. He was going to flee. She ran towards him and he darted away like a hare. It had been years since she'd last hunted and before long she was doubled over, gasping for breath.

She watched him disappear, a grey blob that became one with the leaves as soon as he reached them.

But he'd left his makeshift shrine behind. A handful of flowers – twelve to be exact, arranged in a circle around a peculiar, pyramid-shaped candle.

She scooped them up.

***

When the sun rose again, she heard a mournful horn.

She threw open the hut door to see a small army of Empire soldiers swarming the village common. Some were setting up tents down by the river, while others were felling trees. Their bright steel breastplates glinted with danger in the morning sun, and the smell of metal and sweat was in the air.

Her father pushed past her.

'What's all this?' he demanded. 'What business have you here?'

A hard-faced officer stared him down. 'We've tracked a fugitive to your valley. We're looking for him.'

Nerena immediately knew who they wanted. 'What has he done?' she blurted.

'None of your concern,' the officer said with a pointed glare. 'You have nothing to fear from us. We have our own food and my men won't go near you. But if he knocks on your door, you're to turn him away. Tell him he's not welcome.' He pointed. 'Use those exact words, you hear?'

Her father nodded and the officer moved on.

Once he was out of earshot, he rounded on Nerena. 'What do you know?'

'Nothing,' she said.

He sighed. 'You can't fool me, Nerena. I know you. Have you seen him?'

She shook her head, biting her tongue.

He wiped his face. 'Watch yourself. These men don't know mercy, especially for our kind. We have to look out for ourselves.'

Our kind.

It was the first time she'd heard him speak that way.

***

They ate their last meal of the day in silence, sitting around the hearth. Her mother looked ashen and her father's forehead was etched with frown lines. He pinched his face between his thumb and finger and stared at the wall between bites. Her mother had to prompt him to eat more than once.

After dinner they retired to their beds. Nerena settled under her blanket but kept her dayclothes on. When she was sure they were asleep, she lit the candle and arranged the flowers on the surrounding floor. Each a different colour, each a different type of flower, though she did not recognise them. Flowers from another land, she was sure, but how were they so fresh? They looked as though they'd been picked hours ago.

Deep in the night, she shrugged her cloak on and hurried out, the candle and flowers in her arms.

There were fires burning in the soldiers' camp. Laughter and loud voices echoed up the valley but there seemed to be none in the village. She was still careful, creeping slowly – and only when she was sure the way was clear.

She made her way to the silent stones.

The air was still, expectant – quiet, like it always was. She knelt by the stones and lit the candle, laying the surrounding flowers.

'I'm sorry I took them,' she whispered.

Silence. The stones loomed black above her.

'They weren't for me.'

She looked around. From this part of the mountainside she had a clear view of the soldiers' camp at the mouth of the valley. There were at least twenty fires, twinkling in the dark like stars. That seemed an awful lot of metal to be hunting one man.

As she watched, she heard a rustle. It quickly grew louder. Moments later it was joined by the clattering of metal armour plates, men shouting and screaming. She ducked as what felt like an army swept over her. Weapons smashed against shields and warriors wailed in their final moments, and when she lifted her hands, they were red with blood in the candlelight.

She screamed.

'Shh, do you want them to find you?'

The desperate voice brought her back. All was silent again.

The kindly fugitive stood over her, offering a hand.

Her hand was wet, but only from the dew on the grass. He helped her to her feet.

'What happened?' she said.

'You saw an echo of what came before,' he said with a grave expression. 'The history these stones hold.'

'There was a battle here?'

'Yes,' he said, and his hand moved to his stomach as though tracing the ghost of a wound. 'I was here.'

She scowled. 'Impossible. You're not old enough.'

There was a sad smile on his face, and she realised the wisdom of his eyes betrayed an age more advanced than his skin. 'I see you know nothing of my people. The Empire always said we'd find no welcome here, even in the furthest reaches of the old realm, but I always dared to hope.'

She remembered the officer's words. To refuse him entry, to say he was unwelcome. 'I don't know you, but I welcome you. You can stay in my house if you wish.'

He smiled and his face creased. 'You're kind, but no. I don't wish to put you in danger. Besides, I'm used to the wilds.'

'What are you doing here?' she asked.

He gestured at the candle and flowers. 'These stones hold memories of the past, but the magic only lasts so long.

Someone must sit here and remember, and light the candle. It gives the magic strength.'

She blinked at the man, and her eyes were drawn to the runic tattoos on his arms. Stories weaved into his flesh.

'What are you?'

'I'm a Keeper,' he said with a soft smile and a hint of sadness. 'You've never heard of one.'

She shook her head.

'We are taught the powers of memory magic. To carry, absorb, and send memories. It is a powerful tool, so we are sworn to neutrality. The harm we could do…'

'And you remember the battle for these stones.'

'I remember many things, including memories that aren't my own. But yes, that's why I'm here.'

'What were they fighting for?'

'Your village,' he said with a shrug. 'Empire won in the end, as they won the war. But believe me when I say we tried.' He glanced around at the darkness, the grass and the swaying trees. 'I must be left in peace to finish the ritual. But thank you for your welcome. It means more than you know.'

***

Nerena went to work the field with her father, as she did every day, but she struggled to focus. The battle had left an imprint on her, an image that seemed to exist on the inside of her eyes. The slaughter played in her mind over and over. It made her hands slow and her thoughts groggy. For the first time, she thought about the history of their little valley. A hundred questions filled her mind, and the vision gave her the answer.

Durmedians, they called themselves. Before the Empire came, they were Durmedians.

She was distracted by someone running. They'd come from the neighbouring field and were heavily out of breath. 'Found him,' the young man said. 'They've found him!'

'The fugitive?' her father said.

She was already running.

The soldiers were packing up when she reached the common. The officer gave her a sharp smile as she rushed past.

Two young men in uniform were dismantling a guillotine frame. A red spray on the ground betrayed their act.

She couldn't look. Her stomach turned.

'Nerena,' her father said and placed a hand on her shoulder. She shrugged it off and ran home, head down to hide her reddening face and the tears in her eyes.

Inside, a light made her pause.

There, beside her bed, was the pyramid-shaped candle, flickering slightly in the breeze blowing in from outside. Around it were the twelve flowers, arranged in a perfect circle.

As she watched them, memories filled her head.

And she knew what she had to do.

THE MOSS BARON

Talfrin's sword belt rattled as he walked.

The hills were covered with pale grass, punctured occasionally by boulders and rocky ridges. Behind the clouds, the white glow of the sun was sinking closer and closer to the horizon.

It would go dark soon.

A twinge of pain shot through his back. It wasn't as easy as it was in his youth, this travelling. The weight of his shield and supplies, both lumped on his back along with his steel sword, was taking its toll on him. And his feet were aching despite the new boots. *Especially for warriors*, they'd told him. *Your feet will never tire.* What horseshit. He should've bought that old mule instead. Then it could have carried his pack, and at least he'd have had company.

They called it the shield road. The path of the lone warrior, forced to carry their own supplies. He'd walked it for too long.

How many days had it been since he'd seen another traveller? At least two. And perhaps a fortnight since the last village. There was no disputing it, he was in the land of the moss barons now.

His hand flickered over his sword's hilt by instinct. There was no law here beyond the tip of one's own blade. A second's lapse in concentration could mean death. Which was why, whenever there was a fork in the road, he chose the open path. It was safer to be surrounded by nothing. It was colder – the wind was strong – but at least he could see someone coming.

The rugged landscape reminded him of the Frendic Hills. They were miles and miles away, but he missed them now. That was where Kadahrn, the home of the Bladekin, was. He missed the open fires and the big dinners prepared especially for them as they underwent their vigorous training.

One day, he would return.

The ancient path climbed a small hill, causing him to work up a sweat. He brushed the hair out of his eyes – black, shoulder-length hair scored by a streak of grey. The valley below went on for what seemed like miles. Not a single farm, house or settlement in sight. *Another night under the stars.* At least he had his tent.

He stopped to enjoy the view, his blue-and-white-checked cloak tugged by the wind. The road ahead slowly wound back down into the valley.

Something caught his eye.

Is that a fire?

He smiled. Looked like he would have company this evening after all. As he drew closer, he saw there were at least two tents, though he caught no glimpse of movement. He comforted himself with the thought of warm food and a peaceful night's sleep – he never slept comfortably alone in the wilds, always afraid something would creep up on him.

'Hail,' he said as he approached. There was no response.

Strange. Perhaps they were using the final hours of daylight to hunt or forage?

The tents were simple, like his own: leather sheets laid over wooden frames, a bedroll and cleared earth inside. They stood either side of the fire, which was encased in a ring of earth. Beside the fire was a large rock with a flat top, which he perched on with a grunt. He dropped his things on the ground and relaxed.

If all went well, he'd reach Riburh in the next day or so, but it was impossible to be sure. The scrawled map they'd given him was barely legible. As far as he could tell, he was on the right road.

He rubbed his face. Working for a moss baron. How had it come to this?

At least it would be an adventure.

Rustling came from behind him. He hopped to his feet, drawing his sword and turning with lightning speed. A bearded man wearing ragged furs stared back at him, wide-eyed.

'The fuck you doing here?' the man said.

'I wanted a place to rest for the night.'

The man aimed his sword at Talfrin, his hand flexing on the old leather straps. 'The only thing stopping me right now is that tattoo.' He pointed with the blade. 'You really a Bladekin?'

He was pointing to the inky sword on Talfrin's left cheek, its blade facing down. Sometimes he forgot it was there. 'I am.'

The man licked his lips, then lowered his weapon. 'I don't want an early death. Camp here if you like, but these tents are ours. What's your name?'

'Talfrin. Yours?'

'Rikker. Well, Talfrin, do what you like. I ain't gonna stop you.'

'You want me to take a night watch?'

Rikker chuckled. 'No chance. You can go find firewood, though.'

Talfrin didn't move.

Rikker shrugged. 'So what're you doing out here? Doesn't a Bladekin have better places to be?'

'I need the money,' he said – which wasn't a lie. But it wasn't the whole story, either.

The man looked almost sympathetic. 'Don't we all. Least having that tattoo you know no-one's gonna rob you.'

Talfrin smirked. There was no need to ask what the man did for a living. The charred bones in the fire told Talfrin he was a poacher. Probably poached the odd traveller too, to make ends meet. 'You know a woman named Sabyne?'

"Course we know her,' another voice said. Talfrin turned to see a tall man with rotten teeth and light blond hair emerge from the trees, a freshly slaughtered hare over his shoulder. 'Her men spend half their time chasing us around the hills.' He dropped his catch and threw a log on the fire.

'Likes to call this her land,' Rikker said. 'Ain't her land, of course. It's the emperor's. But since he don't enforce it, it's no-one's.'

'Which means it's ours.' The other man said.

'Can't argue with that,' Talfrin said.

Both men sat on the ground, stretching their hands towards the fire. Talfrin watched the flames creep up the log, turning it black.

Rikker was staring at him. 'Why'd you ask about her?'

Talfrin met his stare. 'I have business with her.'

'What kind of business?'

'What business do Bladekin usually have?'

Rikker kept his eyes on him. 'I dunno. Don't know much about them. Heard rumours, though.'

'What kind of rumours?'

'I heard of one who travelled a thousand miles to settle a grudge. They're single-minded, trained killers.'

Talfrin smiled. He was incorrect, but Talfrin was happy to let him believe it.

Rikker settled into a dark frown. 'Just my luck. The only Bladekin in the whole Mosslands, and I find him in my camp.'

'I'll be gone by morning.'

There weren't many words after that. Talfrin watched as the sun crept towards the horizon, turning the sky red. When the fire was hot enough, the men set up a small frame and started roasting a hunk of venison. Talfrin watched them silently as the air filled with the scent of roasting flesh.

At times like this he'd usually read, but he didn't trust these men. Rikker gave him a dark look when he thought Talfrin wasn't looking.

Maybe he wouldn't sleep tonight after all.

'We're gonna need more wood,' Rikker said to his friend. 'Bladekin, you fancy doing some work yet?'

Talfrin shrugged and grabbed the axe without a word. The wilds suddenly seemed like a nicer place to be.

He took his shield and pack. The men didn't meet his eye.

The Mosslands were rather beautiful in the dusk. A rough, frontier kind of beauty, like his native Tovenar. He took his time, sauntering slowly through the trees. Finding a few thick, dead branches, he started splitting them. Slowly, methodically, without breaking into a sweat. He'd only need enough for one, anyway.

When he returned to the camp in the early dusk, it was deserted. Both tents were gone and they had kicked dirt over the fire. A smile spread across his face.

***

Whatever their motives, the men had covered their tracks well.

No doubt Rikker had been planning his exit from the moment he saw the Bladekin tattoo. Talfrin hadn't realised until much too late, though. These weeks of travel had dulled his senses.

By dawn, his tent was already packed, the fire buried. He briefly considered tracking them. But they'd be far ahead by now, and he doubted it was worth it. He set off along the road again: Riburh wasn't far now.

A few hours later, he came across the first farm.

A paltry place. The shack was small and old and thoroughly in need of repair. A mud-and-wood wall surrounded two enclosures, one for goats and the other for chickens. To anyone else it would have been a dire sight, but it made him smile.

He passed another half an hour later, and two more after that. The last one lay beside a river. They'd irrigated their fields and were trying to grow crops. The barley stalks were short, the heads small, but they were a welcome sign of civilisation.

A farmer in a simple green tunic was picking through the crop, diligently yanking out any weeds. Talfrin raised a hand to him as he walked and the man returned it.

'This the land of Sabyne?' he asked.

'It is,' the farmer said, resting his hands on his hips. 'Why d'you ask?'

'I need to speak with her.'

'You do, do you?' the farmer said, and raised his hand to get a better look at him. 'You look like trouble to me.'

'I don't cause trouble, I stop trouble.'

The farmer came over, holding out his hand. 'In that case, it's a pleasure to meet you, sir.' They shook hands. He glanced at his tattoo. 'Don't see many of your kind here.'

'I got a letter.'

'From Sabyne?'

'From her court.'

The farmer grinned. 'You'll be here to sort out the monsters, then.'

'I might be,' Talfrin said.

The farmer looked taken aback. 'I'm only joking, son. Some of my goats disappeared some nights back, but I suspect those hill poachers. By the Sky, it could even have been the folks from Riburh. But my wife says she saw monster's eyes in the field.'

'Eyes?'

'Yeah,' the farmer said, looking a little embarrassed now. 'I told her it's probably nothing, but–'

'What colour were they?'

'Uh,' he said, scratching the back of his head. 'She said they was yellow. Like the glow of a lantern. I said they probably was lanterns, but she'd have none of it.'

'Thank you, sir, you've been very helpful.'

'Don't mention it,' the farmer said with a perplexed smile. 'Out here we like to have as little to do with you lot as possible. Outsiders, you know. Emperor ignores us then. So if she's asked for you, something big is going on.'

***

A rocky cliff, roughly eighty feet high, cast its shadow over the road. The fort of Riburh clung to its base. It was simple: a low wooden palisade enclosing half a dozen buildings. Surrounding it was a shallow ditch, and at the corners stood two rickety watchtowers.

Such a place would scarcely have been called a camp back west, but out here in the Mosslands it was an intimidating sight.

The warriors at the gate let him through at once. They were clearly expecting him.

The courtyard was filled with freshly hewn logs and labourers bustling back and forth. A sawmill to his left was turning them to lumber, while others were shaping wood into shields. The air smelled of fresh tree sap and bark.

A dark-skinned warrior leaned against a wall, eyeing him up.

'You expecting a war?' Talfrin said.

He carried on staring. He was a bald man with a pinched face, a hint of cruelty behind his eyes. 'No war. Might be some killin', though. You're Her Lordship's Bladekin.'

'I am.'

He smiled. 'Might be some killin' for you, too.'

The warrior pointed him to a two-storey wooden hall at the far end of the courtyard. It was a haphazard building: the roof was uneven and the right wall slanted inwards. It didn't look like a lord's seat. But looks could be deceiving.

Despite its crudeness, Riburh was crawling with armed men and women, all wearing a red tabard bearing the black head of a wolf on the breast. From the look of them, most were professionals – even if they were hired mercenaries. He suspected folks like the farmer had to pay a hefty tax in return for Sabyne's protection.

Then again, in a land where bandits camped blithely beside the road, perhaps that protection was appreciated.

But even these warriors would struggle to do the job of a Bladekin.

In recent times, Bladekin usually found employment amongst the wealthy lords of places like Guenteria and Gilgara, who wanted their pampered children to be taught how to fight by magic warriors. Rarely did they venture so far east. But the promise of magical treasure had swayed Talfrin.

Because it was the job of a Bladekin to find such things.

He opened the doors and entered the hall of a moss baron.

It was more impressive than he expected. The hall was long and wide, the floor covered by a blue carpet. Tapestries hung from the walls between lit torches. Some bore geometric patterns and bright colours, others the black wolf's head which Talfrin assumed was Sabyne's sigil. In the centre of the room was a hearth-fire lying beneath a slit in the roof for smoke to escape. He took off his boots and crossed the floor barefoot, feeling the soft fibres of the carpet, a luxury he hadn't known in what felt like years.

At the far end of the room was a stone platform on which a throne draped in furs stood. Perched on this throne, flanked by two warriors, was Sabyne.

Her appearance took him by surprise. She was thin, but muscular. Over her fine clothes she wore a bright red cloak – Tovenish wool, judging by the swirling patterns embroidered on it. Her blonde hair was clipped short, her face angular and threatening, her skin ivory. She'd been deep in conversation with her warriors, but stopped to look when the door opened. Her eyes were like a predator's. She watched him approach with a slight curve of her lips.

'You accepted my offer, then.'

He stopped before her throne. 'I didn't.'

'You are bold, to speak to me without using my title,' she said, her face unreadable. 'If you don't accept, why are you here?'

'I'm intrigued. But I never agree to contracts without knowing all the details, my lady.'

'I'm a lord, not a lady,' she said. 'But you speak wisely. I would have thought you a fool if you'd said yes.' Her eyes hovered on him. 'Why do you think I summoned *you* in particular?'

'I doubt it's for my tutoring skills,' he replied.

She laughed. A deep, smooth laugh. Well-practised. 'Do you know much about the Mosslands, Bladekin?'

He grimaced. 'I know it's disputed land.'

'Exactly,' she said with a smile. 'Claimed by the Samerens.'

'I'm a magic hunter,' he said. 'I don't mess with the Empire. Not for any price.' He turned to leave.

'Wait. This is about more than gold.' She leaned on her hand, looking at him with those wolf eyes. Squaring him up. 'I will explain, but you must give me chance to speak. If you'd accompany me upstairs?'

'Are you sure that's wise, Your Lordship?' one of her warriors said.

She stood, ignoring them. 'Come, Bladekin.'

Talfrin followed her through a side door and up some carpeted stairs. At full height she was taller than him.

He spotted a sharp knife concealed beneath her ruddy cloak.

His senses were sharp as she led him down a corridor and through a set of doors into a private study. This room was much barer than the hall, featuring no furniture at all besides a desk covered in papers. She lit a candle.

'Let me show you this.'

She moved the papers aside and revealed a map. In the centre lay the fort, labelled Riburh. Sprouting from it was a network of roads that led to other marked settlements – tiny hamlets and individual farms like the ones he'd passed. There were roughly twenty of them.

'This is my land,' she said. 'My *demesne*, I suppose you'd call it where you're from. What do you think?'

'I think it's the emperor's land,' Talfrin said.

She bristled. 'Is it? These people pay my tax and feed my court. I protect them from bandits and monsters. You ask them who their lord is, they'll say Sabyne. Ask them who the emperor is and they'll give you a blank stare.'

'That will count for nothing if the emperor's men come knocking.'

'That's it,' she said with a grim smile on her face. 'Look at this place. The dirt barely grows anything and we're surrounded by troll clans. There's probably fewer people living here than in the smallest village in Old Sameren. They don't care about this place, which makes it mine.'

He said nothing.

'Until recently, there was nothing here of any value,' she continued.

'Until recently?'

'Yes. The earth shook last year and there was a landslide. When the dust settled, it revealed a cave. People started talking about seeing figures in the dark, the word "monster" was uttered. Now it's all my people can talk about.'

'The lantern-yellow eyes.'

She blinked. 'That's right. You've already spoken to them.'

'I have.'

'You know what those eyes mean,' she said.

'Sprakes.'

'Yes. And wherever there are sprakes, there's magic.' She rested her hands on the desk, looking at the map. 'It's on everyone's lips. I'm not a fool. I know some of my people are Empire spies. Soon enough, word will get back to the emperor. And they'll be interested in me.'

'You don't know what's in there?'

She smiled at him, the smile of a hunter who has their prey cornered. 'No, but whatever it is, I'll let you have it.'

He smiled, almost a sneer. 'It's not yours to give away. Not in the emperor's eyes. And I've got to go back that way.'

But now she was smirking. 'They don't need to know where it came from. Besides, I can see the greed in your eyes, Bladekin. I know what your type are like. Always hungry for magic. Well, it's yours. I only ask that you show me whatever you find. Take it away, and the emperor will forget about us.'

'Fair enough.'

'You accept?'

He signed her contract.

***

The fort had very few provisions. He visited the only outfitter there, but her goods were old and poorly made. Still, he managed to convince Sabyne of his need for a mount. It was a small horse, mottled grey with a heavy brown snout and knobbly knees. A poor specimen, but not old. He named him Spens.

Spens adapted to him surprisingly quickly. Before long Talfrin was able to take his mind off riding and soak up the atmosphere of the Mosslands.

It was extraordinarily open. Unnervingly so. After spending the last few months in the relatively cramped lowlands of Guenteria, crossing the mountains onto the Steppe had been a shock he still hadn't recovered from. To the east, thousands of miles of flatlands stretched further than any man had ever travelled, wild and roadless, roamed by tribes of trolls and giants who lived off meat and bone.

He thought of the lone farmer beside the road. It had probably been days since he'd last seen another soul.

It made him shudder. If he ever bought a farm, it would be in the heartlands.

The fort receded from view and there was nothing around him but rolling grass alternating green and gold, the occasional tree, and the thin path that snaked between the lumpy hills. Spens was well in his stride now, having found a comfortable walking pace for them both. He pulled out the map and studied the route to the cave.

'Oi! Bladekin!'

The sudden voice startled him, but he knew it immediately.

Turning in his saddle and drawing his blade, he watched as the two bandits crept down from a rocky ridge. He'd missed it entirely: the perfect place to spring an ambush.

'I found your firewood, but you'd already left,' Talfrin said.

'You've been to the fort,' Rikker said, his jaw tight. He glanced at Spens. 'Nice mount.'

Both men were carrying swords on their belts, but Talfrin could handle that easily. It was the bow in the blond man's hand that worried him.

'That means you've spoken to Her Lordship,' Rikker continued. 'And now you're heading east.'

'And now I'm heading east,' Talfrin confirmed.

'That's the wrong way,' Rikker said. 'You came from *that* way. Nothing out there but grass.'

'That's disappointing. I think I'll check for myself, though.'

'What are you hoping to find?' Rikker's skin was pale, his eyes wary. Clearly he'd lost none of his fear of the Bladekin since their first meeting.

Talfrin shrugged. 'Something more interesting than grass.'

'You will if you keep going,' the blond man said and nocked an arrow.

Talfrin sighed. He carefully dismounted, patting the horse's flank. He slipped his sword free of its scabbard.

The bandit loosed the arrow.

It was as though time slowed down. Talfrin watched the dull metal head racing towards him. When it drew near, he stepped aside, sweeping his sword up and slicing the shaft in two. The halves careened through the air, landing in the grass behind him.

'Idiot,' Rikker said. 'Should've just shot him when we saw him.'

'Should've,' the Bladekin said and moved in quickly. The bandit shot another arrow, but this time missed wildly. Then Talfrin was on him.

He went down easily.

Rikker held his sword at arm's length, pointing at the Bladekin's face.

'You killed him.'

'He shot at me.'

The man was trembling all over. 'What are you going to do?'

'I'm going to go into that cave and find that treasure. Are you going to die for the emperor?'

He shook his head.

'Then drop your sword.'

He dropped it.

'If you go back west, the emperor's agents will string you up. Go to Riburh. Sabyne will give you a job. Mucking the stables, most likely, but at least you won't starve.'

The Bladekin returned to the dead man, checking his pockets. He found his money pouch and sliced it open. Out poured a handful of solid gold Sameren coins with the emperor's face on them.

He flicked a single coin to Rikker. 'Rest of these are mine.'

Talfrin mounted Spens and left him there, continuing down the road.

Those bandits could've had him if they'd played their cards right.

It stuck in Talfrin's mind. He'd allowed himself to slip, to stop watching. And it had nearly led to his death. He was lucky the poacher shouted his name, alerting Talfrin to their presence. A silent arrow would have done it.

Maybe he was getting old. Or maybe he'd spent too long in the heartlands. Either way, he wouldn't make that mistake again.

He rode slowly, monitoring every tree and ridge. Sabyne's concerns had been answered. If the Empire were paying bandits for their eyes, they almost certainly knew about the cave. Which meant they'd be getting involved.

But he'd already signed the contract.

He sighed. No matter how hard he tried, he always ended up involved in politics somehow. Even here, at the edge of the world.

As he rode, he sensed the magic of the cave. When he crested the next small hill, he saw it.

A gaping black hole in the side of a sandstone cliff, sitting at the top of a steep slope. The road below was buried beneath rock and dirt.

The average person wouldn't have seen anything out of the ordinary, but part of becoming a Bladekin was learning how to read magic. And magic was pouring out of that hole in the earth.

He dismounted, tying Spens to a nearby tree. From his pack he drew a phial of thick, magical oil. It would be essential. He slung his shield over his back, gripping a torch in his free hand.

***

It took his eyes a while to adjust to the dark.

A shallow stream trickled between the rocks, flowing from deeper in the cave. He trod lightly, following the tunnel as it sloped upwards. He stripped off his cloak and left it on a stalagmite; the air was cold, but very humid. He was already sweating despite the chill.

He'd been in many caves and he'd yet to encounter one he found pleasant. The air was thick and stagnant. The lack of a breeze was dangerous in combat – it was easy to overheat or become dehydrated.

He found the source of the stream – a stagnant pool nestled between some rocks. He knelt, studying the pool's bed: it was soft clay. In it were two footprints.

Footprints with four toes, each with talons on the end.

Now he knew for sure. This was a sprake den.

He took his time clambering over the rocks, making sure not to overexert himself. After all, he knew he wasn't alone now.

Every sound seemed amplified. Each pebble skittering down a slope was like the booming of a war drum. Every footstep felt clumsily loud. He stopped every few metres to listen, hearing nothing but eerie silence.

The cave tunnel widened. Before long he was in a large, echoing cavern.

A stocky round column – roughly eight feet wide – lay directly ahead. Piled around its base were makeshift bedrolls and lean-tos, old blankets and rags and rotting bits of wood.

But there was no sound, no movement, no fire or smell. Perhaps the sprakes had moved on?

Couldn't be too careful. He drew his steel sword, watching for yellow eyes in the dark.

Carved into the column were runes, illuminated by the glow of his torch.

It had been many years since his training, but they looked Old Durmedian to him. Perhaps this was an old tomb of theirs? Though this was a long way beyond their borders.

A croak made him turn.

Standing ahead, wooden spear angled at him, was a sprake.

Its lantern-yellow eyes shone from beneath a heavy, scaly brow. Its long snout was open in a nasty snarl, while its triangular ears were forward and alert. A ragged copper breastplate covered its chest.

As Talfrin moved towards it, sword raised, two more emerged from the dark, warbling from deep within their throats.

The spear jabbed towards him and he twisted aside, lashing out with his free hand to knock the point away. He rushed in and stabbed the sprake through the chest, blue blood spilling over his hand. He let it fall and took a defensive stance, daring them to come to him.

Another sprake leapt at Talfrin with a war axe, screeching with anger. He ducked its attack and drove a fist into its chest, winding it. The third one came at him with the broken half of a sword, lunging towards his face. He caught its wrist mid-stab – the fractured end came perilously close to his eyes. With a rush of strength he forced it back, shoving it to a close distance and writhing to put the point of his sword between them again. Talfrin heard the other sprake rushing from behind and swung quickly: the attack caught it off guard and it fell, clutching its side.

The half-sword sprake dropped its weapon and tackled him, knocking him hard to the stony ground. It groped his face with dry, scaly fingers, pulling his jaw. He lashed out with his foot, but it stayed. The pressure on his jaw grew. Talfrin kicked again, again, until it finally released and he quickly brought his elbow up, knocking its snout aside. It came straight back, this time clamping onto his neck with its teeth. He grasped around for a weapon and found the half sword. The monster hissed in his face and he slashed the saggy skin under its throat, causing it to roll away. He scrambled and retrieved his sword, finishing the creature as it crawled across the floor.

Rolling onto his back, he stopped to catch his breath, his chest rising and falling rapidly. He smiled.

He was getting close.

***

Another tunnel appeared on his left, descending steeply. He sat and listened for a while. The walls reflected his orange torchlight back at him, making it look as though the rocks were glowing with heat.

Was that his imagination? No, the air was warmer here.

He doused his torch and, as he suspected, wasn't thrown into total darkness. There was a distant, fiery glow coming from the new tunnel. He made his way down the steep descent as slowly as he dared, sword at the ready. He followed the curve right, and some way down the new tunnel there was another, branching off to the left.

This time, though, the tunnel had clearly been carved by hand.

It was square, with straight walls and a flat floor. Looking closely he noticed there were faded threads on the ground where a rug or carpet must have once lay.

At the end of the corridor was an old wooden door, wrapped in rusting iron bands and fastened by a thick metal latch. To its side was an iron brazier. Its flames licked the air lazily, leaving black soot stains on the roof and wall.

He froze. The flames moved softly like dancers at a ball, robed in yellow and orange gowns. To anyone else's eye, they would have looked entirely ordinary.

But he knew different.

Pulling the phial and a grubby rag from his pack, he rubbed his sword with the oil.

As soon as the cloth touched the metal, the flames darted towards him. He threw himself to the ground and rolled, springing back up and swinging his sword around.

The fire dodged and attacked his face again, scorching the hairs of his cheeks. Two gaping holes served as its eyes. He lashed out desperately as it came forward, his eyes closed.

He heard a hiss.

The warmth on his face retreated as the fire dwindled, backing into the sooty corner.

He approached it slowly. Even weakened, the fire wraith could still be dangerous. But this one had lost its will to fight. It sat on the stone, eyes now gone. Accepting its fate.

He sheathed his sword.

'Go on, get out of here.'

It didn't move.

'I don't want to kill you. Go on.'

It vanished in a flash of light and heat.

He relit his torch and opened the door.

Within was something that would have astounded his old mentor. His architecture studies came back in a flash: it was undoubtedly of Old Durmedian construction. Thick, stone beams stretched across the roof, carved to look like giant snakes. At the end of the chamber was a high block.

On it was an altar fashioned like a woman's head. Her hair was long, her nose narrow and pointed. Her face twisted in defiance. On her head was a glittering silver crown adorned by three tall points. Twelve purple gems glittered in the torchlight. He knew why: one stone for each Old Durmedian kingdom. Each one was the size of his thumbnail.

An Old Durmedian crown. Talfrin could scarcely believe it. He hesitated to take it.

But he had signed a contract.

***

The doors of the hall burst open and the setting sun cast the Bladekin's shadow long across the floor.

Looped around one forearm was the silver crown.

Sabyne came down from her throne, meeting him halfway across the hall. When she reached him, she bowed. Her warriors shadowed her, moving closer.

'Is that what was in the cave?'

'It is,' he said, and held it out for her to see.

Her eyes were wide. For the first time, she seemed genuinely surprised. She'd dropped her guard. 'A Durmedian crown,' she whispered.

He moved it away. 'It's mine, remember? That was our agreement. And my gold, too, if you please.'

She clicked her tongue. It was a thin tongue, pointed and cruel. Her predator eyes watched him closely. 'Right you are,' she said and clapped her hands. 'Markis, go and fetch the Bladekin his gold.'

'Yes, my lord,' said one warrior.

'Indeed,' she said, turning her attention back to Talfrin. 'That's what we agreed. But surely you'll let me have a look at it?'

'You can already see it,' he said without moving.

She frowned. 'Do you not trust me?'

He glanced at the warriors behind her. Beefy men, kept around because they were the most intimidating in the fort. He could tell they were slow. But he'd struggle against four of them. Their shadows drifted across the floor as the fire in the hearth flickered. The flames danced around each other - slowly, methodically.

Like waltzers at a ball, wearing yellow and orange gowns.

Flames he knew.

His eyes lingered on them.

'I trust you,' he said. 'I trust you to uphold our deal. Which we signed on paper.'

One of the big men sniggered.

'Of course,' she said. 'I don't get to sign many papers out here, so when I do, I mean it.'

He didn't like the tone of her voice.

'So, a crown,' she continued. 'What magical properties does it possess?'

'Who knows? I'll have to test it once I return to Kadahrn.'

Her eyes never left his, not once. They were dark and warm and radiated danger. 'Not even an inkling?'

He took a step back involuntarily. 'I won't know for sure until I've studied it properly.'

She smiled. 'A pity. I knew you were an educated man as soon as I saw you. I just wish you were honest, too. I know Old Durmedian when I see it. I also happen to know a little about Durmedian kings, though I never heard of one who lived in the Mosslands.'

Talfrin said nothing. He made eye contact with one of the warriors. He was tall and bald, with pink ears. His nose was flat, and he looked at Talfrin through his brow. His hand was on his sword.

'It is said they imbued their crowns with the wisdom of their forebears, so they might make better kings. You know your history, Bladekin, and so do I.'

'That changes nothing. We had a deal,' he said.

'I'm afraid I'm breaking our deal.'

Metallic whispers filled the hall as people drew their swords. Talfrin drew his, as did Sabyne.

'I know the emperor owns this land. He has the documents, and paper weighs more than steel in Sameren. But if I have a millennia-old crown, suddenly my claim looks much stronger.'

'Your claim? What do you care about claims?'

'The emperor's men are coming,' she said. 'A little bird told me.'

Talfrin noticed another man in the hall. Hiding behind the warriors, trying not to be seen. A man with a thick, black beard and wide eyes.

'Rikker,' Talfrin said through clenched teeth.

She let the tip of her sword touch his. 'I need that crown, but I don't want to fight you. Lay your sword down and I promise you, once this matter with the emperor's men is settled, you'll go free. With double the coin.'

He looked at the warriors. One or two appeared eager to fight, but the others did not. Some sweated heavily, others licked their lips and couldn't meet his eyes.

He sighed. 'Markis isn't coming back with my gold, is he?'

She shook her head.

He placed his sword on the floor, along with the crown. 'You'd better give me a warm room.'

***

She'd lied. The cell was draughty.

Wind blew through the high window, rattling the wooden door and making his skin prickle. And Talfrin contemplated.

He clasped his head in his hands. He should have cut them down and stole off with the crown, leaving this place to rot.

Or better yet, he should've left the crown in its hole.

If Rikker was to be believed, a hundred Sameren soldiers were heading their way right now.

Sabyne wouldn't give it up without a fight.

He'd failed. Blood would be shed over the crown.

But there had been no way out of that hall without killing. He could have fought those in the hall, and probably the warriors outside, too, and still won. If he slaughtered a settlement for the sake of a magic crown, though, it hardly felt like he was following his code.

He clenched his fist. He had one rule: he didn't get involved in politics. And the emperor's men were coming. This time, he'd sit it out.

He'd sooner flee into the wilds than get caught between two warring factions on the edge of the world.

'Bladekin,' someone said from the other side of the door.

'Yeah.'

The door swung open. It was Rikker.

'What do you want?' Talfrin asked.

He perched on the stool in the corner. 'I just wanted to ask you a few questions.'

'Ah. For Sabyne?'

He looked down, scratched the back of his bald head. 'No, uh, for me.'

The Bladekin folded his arms and leant back on his bed. 'Okay.'

'Well, you're a Bladekin, right? A trained killer?'

'That's right.'

'Why didn't you just kill us? I'm no fool, I know you could've done it. Easily. And I know that crown's worth a pretty penny.'

'I didn't want to spill any blood.'

The man scoffed. 'Sure. You've killed hundreds, why would you stop with us?'

'Never killed anyone who wasn't asking for it.'

'Hmph. And what if the emperor's men come here? Will you fight them?'

'I don't plan to.'

The bandit grimaced. 'If you don't, we hardly stand a chance.'

'That's not my problem.'

'I see,' Rikker said, anger in his eyes. 'Because you aren't cutting someone's throat yourself, you think their blood's not on your hands.'

'These folk follow a moss baron, they know the risk.'

'You say that as though you don't bear any responsibility for this mess.'

'I don't.'

'You do. You're the one who found the crown. The crown makes this place a target, and you and I both know the Empire will burn this place to the ground to find it.'

'Anyone could have found that crown. Even you could've, and I'm sure she'd have sent you if I hadn't said yes.'

There was silence for a while. 'So it's as simple as that? There'll be a bloodbath and you'll do nothing because you're too afraid to take a stance?'

'I'm not afraid.'

'Then what is it?'

'I can't go against my code.'

He stared at Talfrin, incredulous. 'Code? What code?'

'The Bladekin code. No politics, don't cross blades with Keepers, and seize any magic items you find. This breaks that first rule.'

'Saving people's lives is political?'

'It is when you're killing someone else to save them. You want to save them, get Sabyne to give up the crown. That's what this is. It's all about who has the best claim to this land. It's the definition of politics.'

'That's why she won't let go of the crown,' he agreed. 'And you? What do you want the crown for?'

'I want to hide it.'

He grinned, a grin full of malice. 'Yeah, right. No man can resist the pull of power.'

'I can.'

He shook his head. 'I don't know how else to say it, but they need your help, Bladekin. The Samerens are already through Emperor's Pass. They're in the Mosslands - a hundred trained, proficient soldiers. If you sit back, this place will burn and we'll be at the mercy of the emperor's justice.'

Talfrin leant forward. 'Listen. This has nothing to do with me. Keeping them safe is Sabyne's job. If she turns the crown over without a fight, then the matter will be over. You want my help, there it is: hand over the crown.'

'Sabyne won't,' Rikker said.

'Then the blood's on her hands.'

Rikker was silent for a while. 'I have no more words for you. Without your help, we're fucked.' He stood to leave.

'She sent you, didn't she?' Talfrin said.

He said nothing.

***

Talfrin woke to the sound of people in the courtyard.

He pushed the stool to the wall and stood on it, peering out the window.

The yard was still full of piles of fresh lumber. In a corner, some craftworkers were making shields from it, while a few yards away, some children were painting the new shields red and black.

When he'd arrived, he'd noticed the warriors, but they weren't the only inhabitants of the fort. A mother carried a swaddled child as she brought drinks to some warriors, while in a dusty, grassless clearing, two copper-skinned Guenterian girls – barely older than fifteen – were sparring. He wondered about their lives, and what had brought them so far from their homeland. Beside one watchtower, some people were being drilled in the use of spears and shields. One failed to block an obvious thrust and received a clip around the head as punishment.

They were not fighters.

'Do you think she'll fight with us?' someone was saying below his window.

'Sabyne? Yes. She's like that. Not one to leave her people high and dry.'

'I hope you're right.' Their voice wavered. 'I came here to get away from all this.'

'We all did.'

A pause. 'Where's that Bladekin?'

'Left, by the look of it. Haven't seen him in days.'

They scoffed. 'About right, to drop us in this mess and run for the hills.'

'Outsiders. They're all the same.'

It's not your fault, he told himself. *Not your fight.* The Bladekin code forbade it. Stay out of politics, hunt down the magic.

So often, those two objectives intertwined.

He lay in his bed and slept.

***

'They're here!' a desperate voice cried.

Talfrin leapt to his feet and scrambled onto the stool, looking into the courtyard.

It was full of Empire soldiers, their burgundy tunics poking out from behind thick steel breastplates. Each one wore a wide-rimmed metal helm that glinted in the morning sun.

Sabyne's warriors stood in a cluster to the left. Sabyne was at the front. She was deep in conversation with the Sameren general.

'It was in that cave and it's not there now, so I know it's here,' the Sameren was shouting.

Sabyne's response was too quiet for Talfrin to hear.

'You have two options. You either turn over the crown or we'll torch this place and haul you all back to Bucsvar as prisoners.'

'And if I give you the crown?' Sabyne said.

'If you do, His Majesty will allow you to live in these lands as his allies. You will pay him a trifling sum in return for the Emperor's protection.'

She spat at his feet. Swords were drawn, but the Sameren leader raised his hand and his men backed down.

'I take it you were just clearing your throat,' he said.

Talfrin shook his head. She should have accepted his offer. It wasn't worth the bloodshed.

The courtyard was still strewn with logs and lumber, but scattered here and there were people not involved in the fighting. Children and terrified folk in normal clothes, presumably the families of the warriors, or wanderers who had found themselves here on the edge of the world for a hundred different reasons. They watched from hiding places, some shaking with fear or crying. A black-haired toddler waddled from person to person, wailing. It was still morning, still bitter cold, and some had lit a fire with the fresh wood at the far corner of the courtyard, huddling around it for warmth.

He remembered the fire in the hearth. The fire wraith.

He thought about his code.

And he had a plan.

He removed the pin of his belt buckle and used it to pick the lock on his cell door, finding himself in the prison's stuffy corridor. His belongings lay on a low table by the door: he retrieved them, fastening his sword belt and shield securely. If this worked, he wouldn't have to use them.

He followed the dark wooden corridors that led back to the room where they'd first signed their agreement. The map was still on the table. He went down the stairs to the main hall, which he found deserted. As he expected, the fire hadn't yet burnt out, though it was doing a convincing job of looking like it needed more fuel.

'Hello again,' he spoke to the flames.

They flickered between the white-hot logs, crackling.

'I need your help. I'm going to save these people.'

The flames suddenly flickered higher; embers blew over him, causing him to shelter behind his cloak.

'Listen. You don't want people messing with you, do you? If we don't fix this, a lot more people are going to be interested in this place. Your cave won't be safe. But I have an idea that'll send them away.'

Two black holes appeared in the flames. The fire wraith observed him carefully.

'You want your crown back?'

'*Code.*' The voice hissed in his mind, like droplets of water hitting open flames.

'I'm sure some other Bladekin will come after it, in time,' he said. 'I'll put it back. Are you ready?'

It blinked slowly.

'Follow my lead.'

***

Every eye in the courtyard turned to see Talfrin wreathed in flame.

A Sameren warrior yelped in terror. Another dropped her sword.

Sabyne and her warriors backed slowly away. The Bladekin made eye contact with her. She looked stunned, but she gave a very slight nod.

He stood at the foot of the hall for some time, the flames spinning around him like eels. He pointed his hand into the air and they shot up, exploding above him and causing everyone to scream. They shot back down, swirling around his body in ever-changing colours.

He approached the Sameren general.

'You don't know what you're dealing with,' the Bladekin said.

The man swallowed. 'Your conjurer's tricks won't fool me, Sabyne. Hand over that blasted crown.'

'You don't want that crown,' Talfrin said. He looked up at the general through his eyebrows, and knew that his face, wrought in smoke and fire, must have been a terrible sight.

'I think I do,' the general spat. 'I have my orders right here.'

'If you follow them today, they'll lead to your death. That crown is cursed. You touch it, your fingers will burn off.'

The general gave him an insolent smile. 'You sure?'

The Bladekin nodded.

'Let's see about that. I'm done playing games. Take the crown from the moss baron. Go on, move it!'

The Sameren warriors closest to him hesitated, but moved towards Sabyne. As soon as the first stepped within five feet of her, the fire wraith slammed into the ground, cracking the earth and leaving a small crater, sending fire and clumps of earth spraying over them. They stopped in their tracks.

Talfrin saw the anguish on the general's face. He stared him down, hatred bubbling behind his eyes. 'Go on, swords, take the crown.'

His soldiers did not move.

'I said take the fucking crown.'

Still, no-one moved.

'This place is protected by the spirits of Old Durmedia,' the Bladekin uttered in his best doomsaying voice. 'These people are under their protection. You tell your emperor he wouldn't take this land with a hundred thousand men.'

The general ran towards Sabyne.

The fire wraith leapt from Talfrin and engulfed the general. He swatted at the flames as he stumbled away, falling to the ground with desperate wails and rolling. The others stared wide-eyed at their burning comrade. One doubled over, bile spilling from his mouth.

The general stopped moving. A horrid, bitter smell filled the courtyard as smoke softly rose from the officer's flesh.

'Get out of here,' the Bladekin said to the rest.

They fled.

***

The moss baron fulfilled her promise. She paid the Bladekin twice the original amount and let him go. She even gave him Spens, but she insisted on keeping the crown.

He rode off down the road as though he intended to leave. But he'd made a promise to the fire wraith, and it was still whispering in his ear.

He set up camp just beyond the first hill. Here, her warriors wouldn't be able to see the glow from his fire. He warmed his hands on the flames, glancing at the surrounding darkness. Spens snorted.

He hated camping alone. But then, he wasn't alone.

'I made a promise, I know,' he whispered to the fire. 'And I intend to keep it.'

It was a few hours after dark and the moon was high in the sky when he rose from his tent and walked back to the fort.

The fort was silent, though he saw two men on the walls. He watched them for a long time, learning their routine. When one of them disappeared, he scrambled up the palisade, dropping silently into the courtyard. From there he crept to a pile of lumber and moved some planks beneath the window of his cell. He climbed in.

The crown was resting on her throne.

He looped it around his arm and fled into the night.

Back west, he thought. He'd take a well-paid tutoring job, coaching the son of a nobleman in tournament etiquette. If he ever came back this way, it would be for a chestful of gold.

The fire wraith followed him back to the cave. It lit the way to the burial chamber. Down in the bowels of the earth, he placed the crown back on the altar, turned away, and left it there.

THE MOONBLADE PRINCESS

Nadina glimpsed the castle through a gap in the fog. It stood on the edge of a cliff, its stone foundations sinking into the earth. Its towers, thin and knobbly like old fingers, raked the dusky sky. The narrow windows were dark; they had been for years.

This was the place.

She pulled her black cloak tighter around her as rain pelted down. Despite the weather, she smiled. Between the fog and the storm, she would be all but invisible. The beasts that stalked such desolate places would never see her. So long as she was quiet, she could focus on the task at hand.

Still, she adjusted her belt and made sure her knife was easily within reach. No need to take any chances.

She left the old shepherd's path, cutting straight across the barren, rocky highland. Lonely, twisted trees clung to mossy rocks, and clusters of brambles with inky berries huddled in the shadows of cliffs, tugged by the wind.

How many years had it been since someone last walked here?

The damp grass knotted around her feet as though it were trying to pull her down. She stepped carefully: this was not the place to rush. All the while she monitored the boulders and ridges that surrounded her, watching for the telltale flicker of a black shape – or the gleaming eye of a lantern – that would betray a trap.

She saw none.

As she passed beneath a lichen-covered overhang, the wind suddenly picked up. Carried on it, between the gusts, she caught faint whispers. She couldn't make out the individual words, but there was a sharpness to them that cut like a blade.

She stopped, drawing her knife, and sheltered beneath the overhang. A cluster of figures stalked along the top of a far hill. They had long snouts and stooped backs, and they were heading towards the castle.

She grimaced. She'd hoped the castle would be abandoned. But that would have been too easy.

Moving to the other side of the ridge, where she could stay out of sight, she watched the creatures. There were half a dozen of them - scaly, reptilian creatures with thin limbs and loping strides, their eyes glowing yellow in the dark. They gripped simple spears, branches with sharpened rocks bound to their ends.

She waited for them to disappear. It was a good sign, though. Sprakes were drawn to places that harboured magic.

Following a dirt path that emerged from a cluster of wild weeds, she headed towards the castle.

She knew this place. She'd been here before. It felt as though it were yesterday, though she knew it was many years ago. She could see it in her mind's eye: the castle grounds which stretched for miles, the neatly-kept grass dancing in the sun. The rose beds and herb gardens full of chives and thyme and sage. She remembered rooting around for mushrooms and wild garlic in the woodland her father kept for his bondsmen, and the smell of freshly sawn lumber hit her nostrils as though she was there again. The rounded vowels and half-consonants of the groundskeeper's heavy accent as he called after her, trying to usher her home as the last rays of sunlight tickled her evening gown, the hem laced with mud.

She wondered what had become of him.

Back then the castle had been a glorious place. Its walls gleamed white in the sun, and bright tents always surrounded its base, pitched in preparation for some tourney or feast. Her father had always known how to impress.

How had it fallen into such disrepair?

Perhaps she'd have to come back, once all this was over. See what she could do to save it.

For now, she prayed the inside was still untouched. That the thing she sought most desperately hadn't been taken.

As she drew closer, the dirt road turned to cobbles. The old towers loomed over her, the plaster flaking off. Water had blackened the stone, and in places, eroded it entirely.

Distracted, she tripped on a cobblestone, grazing her palm. She watched the blood bead, two red dots that looked like eyes. It taunted her. It knew why she was here.

She had no protection, no magic shield – unlike her brother. As heir apparent, their father had sought the greatest wizarding minds and devised a concoction which granted him rapid healing.

She couldn't say they'd never exploited it. She and her brother, Roltast, would spar in the castle courtyard as part of their training. They moved to iron swords much sooner than they should have, and Frinda, their swordmaster, turned a blind eye.

They pushed it too far. She recalled picking the lock on the study door, both of them giggling as they shoved their way in and dug through every drawer and cupboard in the room. They found a strange old sword whose blade was white like the full moon and went to spar with it.

Rubbing her thigh, she felt a phantom pain. She could still see the wound.

She'd been too eager.

Frinda's shouts still echoed in her mind as she hurtled out of the castle towards them, the castle's healer hurrying close behind.

The blade cut him deep, and it never fully healed. It seemed he was not immune to wounds from magic blades.

Fortunately, such weapons were rarely seen.

The front entrance was not a good idea. She didn't want to run into the sprakes. But she knew the castle, and there was more than one way in.

She left the path, venturing partway down the hill so the castle loomed above.

Huddled against the cliff was a cluster of makeshift tents made from sheets of old linen. She approached with her knife drawn, her footfalls disguised by the rain.

They were empty, abandoned. But on the inside of one, someone had left a message daubed with ash.

Burn the king.

Refugees, she assumed. From the north, which had suffered most at the hands of the king's soldiers. It was one of their refrains.

She felt a pang of sadness for them. Such things never used to happen, not before his reign.

Their kingdom was falling into ruin.

Continuing on, she came within view of the familiar stream that trickled by the base of the cliff. Above it, embedded in the dirt, was a round tube of stone, covered by a rusting iron grate. She and Roltast used to use it all the time to sneak in and out after hours. She remembered helping him arrange his meeting with a girl from the village – the first girl he really knew.

Some days later, she was the first girl Nadina knew, too. Lyra, her name was. In the end, she stopped seeing Roltast, choosing to spend all her time with Nadina. Her brother spent months brooding over it.

Simpler times.

She wondered where Lyra was now.

The rusty iron crumbled at her touch. When she tried to open it, the hinges gave way and the entire frame fell with a crash.

Following the old route through the tunnels was easy – she hadn't forgotten a thing. Back then, she used to pretend she was a rat, and the only thing she had to worry about in life was scavenging scraps of food and avoiding people. She indulged in that fantasy now and for a moment, everything was simple again.

She'd always sympathised with those who had little. The rats, the pigeons, the flies. And now, the people of the kingdom, too.

She climbed a ladder and emerged in the kitchens. Webs criss-crossed the room, and insects had eaten the wooden surfaces. A room which had smelled of breakfast and fresh fruit now stank of rotting wood.

It wasn't far to the throne room.

Against the far wall the tall, silver-plated throne still stood proud, though black, tarnished patches were beginning to swallow it. That boded well, at least. It hadn't been looted. She stopped for a while, remembering. This hall had, in its time, been full to bursting with people from across the land, there to petition her father on all manner of things. He'd listen to everyone, for hours each day.

That was what a true king looked like.

She froze when she caught the whispers on the air again.

There was no use lingering.

She passed through the hall, entering the private corridors they'd haunted as a family, seeing the bedrooms of their most trusted servants. She knew where she was going.

Before the door of the old study, she stopped. Tried the handle. Locked. *Of course.*

She drew a lockpick and worked it open, feeling the intimate click of every tumbler, remembering each one.

The portrait above the fireplace caught her eye. Her father, with his thick, red beard, the crown perched perfectly on his head. His enormous arms rested around his children: her to his left, a shy smile on her face, and Roltast to his right, wearing his medal and the delicate tiara of the crown prince.

How different this all could have been. If only she'd been the eldest.

Her eyes lingered on her brother's. Pale green, so calm, so gentle. He'd always been a circumspect man, wise and forgiving.

Oh, big brother, what happened to you?

She steeled herself. Bigger things were at stake here.

She dug through every drawer and cupboard, growing increasingly frantic.

It had to be here. After all this.

An old roll of vellum called out to her. She pulled it out, caressing the surface. Soft, but there was something hard within.

She unrolled it to reveal the old sword, the moon-white blade still pristine, its edge as sharp as it had always been.

Her brother's picture seemed to watch her. His green eyes seemed harsher now. Cold, mistrusting. Afraid.

She slid the blade into her waiting sheath.

A WITCH WALKS

A witch with long white hair and a scar at the right corner of her mouth shivered as she followed the unending stretch of road.

This part of the Old North Road was empty for miles yet, and the sun had dropped from the sky.

But she kept walking.

Her feet had blistered and bled, but she walked.

Her thigh muscles were numb, but she walked.

Her shoulder was red and raw where the strap of her satchel had rubbed it, but she walked, following the glow of her moongem.

Its pulsing was quicker.

Perhaps it knew.

She thought back on that night in the cabin. The night the couple visited her, looking for potions. It warmed her heart.

She'd known they needed her. But she'd needed them, too, and that truth had eluded her.

Too long in her own head, her own routine.

Rensa had asked her about memory magic. And after so many years, the witch had gone to find it.

She remembered the altar, the vision. The burning city.

She walked faster.

There was an imbalance in the world.

A Keeper had broken their oath.

Someone else would have to, as well.

She remembered the high walls of Kadahrn, deep in the highlands. The shrugging and the averted eyes of the Bladekin there. Even the scholars. They wouldn't hear her.

'We have to follow the code.'

Useless.

But the witch could see another.

An itinerant Bladekin, following the road on the back of a knobbly mare. Going west.

His heart wasn't right yet.

But it would be.

She walked faster.

A BLADEKIN STOPS

Talfrin stepped over the threshold, removing his blue-and-white-checked cloak and hanging it on a hook. He asked for a room and a drink and sat up late in the hall, the malty ale teasing his mind into sweet calm.

This was not the time to approach him.

Someone tried it anyway.

The Bladekin looked down on the thin, bedraggled man who tugged his arm.

'Go away.'

'Are you a Bladekin? A real one?'

'I said: go away.'

'I need your help. I've come from Thrynn.'

The man was persistent, he'd give him that.

'I'm not taking jobs right now.' The Bladekin pulled out a letter bearing a swishing signature and a noble seal. 'I have a commission.'

The bedraggled man bit his lip, but didn't leave. 'What's it doing?'

'A cosy job in Gilgara, protecting villagers from sprakes. Just my speed.'

'This is much bigger than that.'

'I don't want bigger. I want to rest.'

The man had thin, brown hair and a bald spot. His chin was short, his jaw fat, and his nose big and round. The type who, usually, would be more likely to punch someone than talk to them. But his eyes glittered and a tear trickled down his cheek.

'There's some evil magic in my kin, sir, and we don't know where to turn. My family are haunted by images at night.'

'Dreams?'

He nodded.

'A disease of the mind. You can see the apothecary for that.'

The man shook his head fervently. 'No, sir, we tried. The dreams are still there. Besides, we're sound in the head, and it happened to all of us at once.'

The Bladekin spun on his stool to face the man, his teeth bared. 'I see you won't take no for an answer. Very well. What are these dreams you're haunted by?'

'Fire,' the man said, his voice cracking. 'Our house burning. They wake my wife many times a night, always screaming. She fears for our children.'

'Have any of you been in a fire recently?'

'No, sir. Nothing of the sort.'

'Have you spoken to anyone else about this?'

He nodded. 'The folks at the city library.'

'And what did they say?'

'Well, sir, they… they said it sounds like memory magic.'

The Bladekin turned back to his drink and took a gulp, saying nothing.

'Sir?'

'I'm done with you. I don't play games.'

The man crept closer, desperation shining in his eyes. 'Games, sir? I'm not playing games!'

'There's no memory magic in Thrynn.'

'How should you know?'

'Because very few people know that magic, and they don't go near cities.'

The man begged, but the Bladekin ignored him. After a while, he retreated to his room to drink in silence. Once midnight passed, he slept, and dreamt of peaceful things.

GULLBARREL

The lights of Thrynn sparkled in the distance. Axi smiled. How long had it been since she'd seen them? Her pack felt lighter already, and the weariness of the last few weeks of travel fell away. She wouldn't be here long, of course. She still had far to go. But she was excited, and as the cart rumbled along the road, her mind scurried down the alleys and backstreets of Portside, already slipping into carefree memories of childhood.

She could afford to spend a few nights here. Wander the old streets, see what had changed. Besides, she needed a few nights in a proper bed. Sleeping pressed up against a dozen other travellers every night was wearing on her. She was sure she smelled more of them than herself.

The cart hit a rut in the road and rattled, jolting them all. She wriggled her legs, which were beneath a sleeping man's arm.

Yes, a few nights in an inn would do her good.

What had become of her old corner, where she used to bed down for the night?

'Thrynn,' said the leader of the caravan, Meilisik. She had dark eyes and a tight bun on her head, and she walked ahead of the cart, leading the horses. 'Port of Guenteria, pride of the Woldlands. A total shithole. I'm leaving tomorrow – if you want to stay, you'll have to find another escort.'

'It's not that bad,' the man beside her whispered, his breath stinking of infected gums and sweet rum. 'There's good fun to be had, if you know where to look. Cheapest in the Three Kingdoms. Might be work there for you, too.'

'I don't think so.'

She leaned away. Another bump in the road made the cart roll, and the man tumbled into her lap. He tried to right himself, arms flailing; a yellowed hand landed on her thigh.

'Sorry, ma'am –'

She didn't give him the pleasure. Shifting her weight, she slammed a fist into his stomach and moved away, so she was standing on the cart. She swept her cloak aside, letting them all see the flash of metal at her hip. If they looked closely enough, they'd have seen the sparkle of mail beneath her jerkin, too.

The folks around them – who had been hidden under their blankets and cloaks, most of them sleeping – blinked at her with alarmed eyes or tried to move away.

The man grimaced, hands outstretched towards her as though he were begging for coin. 'Please, I meant you no harm –'

'Another word, and I'll throw you off this cart.'

He wobbled, blinking slowly, and for a moment she wondered if he even understood what she said. But then he grunted and waved his hand, crawling to the back of the cart – as far from her as possible.

She straightened her cloak and sat. Suddenly, she had much more room than before.

***

They passed through the gate, the wardens standing aside as soon as they saw their caravan. Meilisik tipped her head to them and they returned the gesture. In the torchlight Axi saw a smile on their faces. They clearly knew Meilisik.

Axi noted the livery they wore. Midnight blue tabards, bearing a grinning crescent moon on the chest. The banners that hung from the gatehouse bore the same sigil.

The arms of Lord Bedivar and his family.

During her childhood spent lurking in alleyways, she'd learned to watch for the eyes of the moon on a warden's torso and move the other way. Now, they were a strangely nostalgic sight.

The caravan drew to a halt just after the gates. One by one, they hopped down. Axi smiled when her feet hit the cobblestones. The high street stretched away and curved right, towards the market square. The ancient beams of long-windowed houses jutted over the street, the flicking light of the streetlamps reflected on their undersides.

The passengers huddled together in the face of this big city, unsure where to go. Axi, though, set off straight away, following a narrow street she remembered from years before. The first rule of the urchin life: get off the street after dark. Fortunately, she knew a place. As quickly as that, she was that same urchin she'd been twelve years ago.

She ducked down familiar streets in search of an inn she remembered. She noticed subtle differences: where some buildings had once stood, there were now empty spaces, some overgrown, some charred. Amongst the buildings of the main streets, there were occasional bright, freshly painted houses, with elaborate glass windows and metal guttering. Newly built.

She followed the scent of sewage and sweat into the Portside slum. Here, there were no burning streetlamps. The cramped streets were dark and muddy, and she walked faster.

The Old Rest was an inn she'd worked often as a child, creeping into the private rooms of passed-out drunks and stalking pockets in the main hall. Since then, its foundations had slumped even further forward, so the threshold was buried under packed earth and the roof was nearly touching the building across the street. The cross-hatched, green glass windows glowed a sickly colour because of the warm candlelight within. Some panes were missing, replaced by hasty boards. A fraying rope hinged the door, leaving it swinging at an angle.

Not much had changed. But a new banner hung in one of the windows bearing the head of a fox. It leered at her, its eyes distorted by the bowed, green glass.

She didn't recognise the sigil, but even as a child, she remembered the innkeep saying the Old Rest was not a place for politics. That was different, at least.

Sure enough, the innkeep was a new person, a swarthy woman with heavy brows and cold eyes. She watched Axi with suspicion.

'Ale or beer?' she said unkindly.

Axi asked for beer. 'And a room, if possible.'

She squinted at her. 'A room? Try the waterfront inns, they're more suited to your kind.'

'My kind?'

'Bandits.' She spat the word.

'I'm no bandit!'

'I see your blade,' she said with a flick of her eyes. 'And your mail. Take your trouble away with you.'

'I'm a mercenary by trade.'

The innkeep raised her eyebrow. 'A mercenary.'

'Yes,' Axi said, unable to hide her irritation. 'A real one. Not an outlaw, I don't rob people. I fight for people who can pay me.'

'You fight for Lord Bedivar?'

'Not currently.'

'Would you?'

'If the coin was right.'

She smiled, but the coldness remained in her eyes. 'Right enough. Like I said, you might try the inns in the waterfront.'

The skin of her neck prickled. She turned to see half a dozen folks scattered around the inn now watching her closely.

She suppressed a shiver.

'Might I finish my drink first?'

'By all means.'

She dropped into a rickety chair at a table marked by knife blades and spilled alcohol. Glancing around the room, she noted how the people shuffled, evading conversations with those mere inches for them, apart from to utter a 'sorry' for an accidental bump. Most were lost in their thoughts, minding their own business and enjoying the warmth of an indoor place as a frosty night fell.

No doubt many were planning to sleep in the hall through the night. Perhaps she could blend in, sneak a night anyway. But there were several pairs of eyes still on her.

Beside the bar, there was a huddle of armed men and women who were already deep in their cups. The innkeep served them readily, drink after drink. One's jerkin was torn, and the fabric beneath was ash grey, bearing that same leering fox sigil. Axi grimaced.

She knew every inch of the walls in this place. Countless hours she'd spent here, watching pockets. And now she'd never felt more out of place. Soldiers would never have been welcomed here back in those days. And these were foreigners, she assumed, wearing the sigil of another lord from another land.

The city had changed.

The sooner she made it to Nenraeda, the better. She needed the guiding hand of a drillmaster again, the comfort of other warriors to spar with and build back her skills. The road was exhausting, and her skills were rusty. And this hadn't been as pleasant as she'd expected.

Perhaps she wouldn't stay more than a night, after all.

'The Fox watches.'

The words nearly made her fall out of her chair.

An old man leant on the table beside her, buried in a thick coat. His deep hood made his face all but unseeable in the dim glow of the candlelight, but his flesh was stone grey.

'What are you talking about?'

'The Fox watches,' he said again, and she caught the glint of his eyes. 'He needs warriors to help his return.'

'I'm not in the habit of backing pretenders.'

'The Fox is no pretender. He's the rightful lord of this city.'

'There is no Fox.'

He leaned in, and she saw the reflection of embers in his eyes, though there was no fire behind her. 'Are you so sure?'

'Lord Bedivar is the rightful lord of this city,' she said. 'His family have reigned for generations. Your Fox is nothing more than smoke.'

The man bristled at that, levelling her with an intense glare. 'He is much more than smoke. And he's looking at you, Axi.'

He swept back into the crowd. Axi shivered.

How did he know her name?

She downed her drink and left, fast.

The man's face haunted her thoughts as she made her way deeper into Portside. The glower of those eyes from beneath that hood stuck with her. She glanced over her shoulder, expecting to see him, but she was alone.

The scent of fish and salt and the sound of waves swashing told her she'd reached the Waterfront. She stumbled through the door of the nearest inn, the Gullbarrel. A kindly, bearded innkeep smiled at her across a deserted room.

How late was it?

'Looking for a room?' he asked. His voice was calm, friendly.

In the corner, a midnight blue shield bore a white, crescent moon with a cunning eye and a slice of a grin. That was a comfort.

'Depends. Are mercenaries welcome here?'

'Of course,' he said with a frown. 'Why wouldn't you be?'

'I had some trouble finding a place tonight.'

Something about the man made her trust him. She spilled her story. The Old Rest, the soldiers, the fox and the innkeep and the hooded man. When she was done, tears glistened on her cheeks, which irritated her. It was nothing to cry over. But something about his fiery eyes had spooked her.

The old man rubbed his chin, his snow-white brows knotted in a deep frown. When he spoke, he spoke quietly. 'I'm sorry that happened to you. I'll give you the attic room, it's the safest.' He waved his hand when she offered coin. 'No need. You're one of the good ones. There are precious few in this city these days.'

She stumbled into the small, dusty room, her muscles aching. She collapsed onto the bed and rested.

She saw his fiery eyes.

Her thoughts blurred.

***

She was the height of a man's waist. Darting between the tables, she imagined herself as being like a hare, ready to dash away at the first sight of trouble. She eyed the pockets of people who passed and listened for the telltale chink of gold.

There, a target. A large, bearded man, hemmed in by the crowd and unsteady from drink. She swept in without thinking, her lithe hand snatching his pouch. She was three steps away before he noticed.

'Thief!'

He thundered after her, shoving people aside.

She sped up when she heard the whisper of a blade being drawn.

Out into the street and darting right, she ran as fast as she could. It was a path she'd used before: up ahead was a network of tight alleys, and once she reached that, she was away.

But the man was quicker than she expected, and people clogged the path – more people than usual. Packed shoulder to shoulder, they were all watching the road as though they were waiting for someone.

The crowd slowed her down. She glanced behind and saw his red face, the glint of the blade, as he stalked between the bodies looking for her.

She wriggled away from the alleys, pushing between peoples' legs, trying to get to the road.

Bursting through and falling onto the cobbles, the city erupted in noise.

A horse screamed nearby and hooves stamped the stone, making her instinctively roll away. A pair of rough hands grabbed her shoulders, wearing leather gloves that reeked of urine.

'No! Let her go!' A voice said. It was calm, authoritative, even in the midst of the chaos.

When she finally opened her eyes, she was looking at a tall man. His long black hair was swept back from his pallid face, which was dominated by a hooked nose that made him look like a crow. Around his neck dangled a sparkling, silver pendant – a fox flanked by crow's wings, its eyes two bright orange gems.

He smiled and offered her a hand. She took it.

'My lord,' a soldier whispered, who wore the fox on his livery. 'She's a commoner.'

'What does it matter?' he said, as he stooped to pick her up in his arms. The crowd gasped. His cold lips planted themselves on her forehead, and a spattering of applause broke out. The lord smiled.

Her hunter was not clapping. He was still red-faced, sword drawn. And he seemed not to care who the lord was, because he came forward anyway, prompting the soldiers to block his way.

But the lord was undeterred. 'What's the matter there?' he said.

'That girl is a thief. I want her hands.'

'You'll not have her hands,' the lord said, his voice steady. 'What is it she owes you?'

'I don't give a shit about the coin,' the man said. 'I have plenty more. I want to see justice.'

'I will repay your debt, or you will go about your day. You shan't hurt the child.'

A heavy silence filled the street, the kind which often preceded a thunderstorm. Nobody seemed to move. The man's nose twitched, his teeth baring, as he seemed to think of a response. He drew in a breath.

'A lord is supposed to keep justice. Why else should we have them?'

The crowd hissed.

Axi felt the lord's body tense up at his words, his hands gripping her body a little too tight.

The large man seemed to realise he'd pushed his luck too far. His mouth flapped and he took some steps back. A soldier stepped forward, the point of his spear dropping to chest height.

'Let him go,' the lord called in his calm, soothing voice.

But when he leaned over to the soldier beside him, his voice seethed with malice.

'See that he burns tonight.'

As she drifted back from the dream, she could see with her adult mind the lord had only treated her so kindly because he was being watched. There was a fiery anger in his eyes, the kind which lives only in the most evil of men.

But he smiled when he looked at her. 'What's your name?'

'Axi.'

She knew his face. The curve of his jaw. The pale, grey skin.

The hooded man from the inn.

When she awoke, her body was shaking. Heavy drops of water were pelting her skin, and her clothes were stuck to her. Her hair was sodden.

She was standing in the middle of the street, the same street she'd ran to in the dream. Now, though, the buildings had slumped slightly, and the mud seemed to have crept up their foundations a few inches.

Shouts broke her trail of thought.

'Fire! Fire!'

A man rushed past her and she caught his arm.

'Where?'

But she already knew the answer.

'The Gullbarrel. Come on, we need every pair of hands!'

TRINKET SHOP

Princess Nadina passed through a market square in a small town in Voleren.

It was noisy, busy. A faire day, when traders from across the kingdom came to hawk their wares.

She hoped she could pass unnoticed.

Because she had something precious to sell. Something that could change the fates of kings.

Something that had tasted royal blood.

She spoke to many, but trusted none. A single stray word could mean her death.

Nadina dodged down a dark alley, hoping to find a trader of secrets.

She found one.

She liked what Nadina had very much. It was the kind of thing that would really interest some of her clients, she said, scratching her rough cheek. And no need to worry, she wasn't on the side of kings.

Nadina had to be rid of it. Purge the evidence of her crime.

She flashed the lunar-white blade. They bartered. Precious objects passed through Nadina's hands like fresh apples and she weighed them up, gauging their worth. Until in her palm sat a shiny, silver thing with two citrine gems for eyes. A fox's face glowered at her with fire.

As she held it, primal anger filled her. A hatred of the world, a desire to see it burn.

And yet she saw something beneath it. A calmness, a sense of purpose. Buried deep. And a pyramid-shaped candle surrounded by twelve fresh flowers. Those thoughts were old, faded, almost gone.

A crow cawed in the distance.

There were many other things she liked better, but that was the object which stuck in her mind when she ventured to the inn that night. She would return in the morning and decide.

But before she could sleep, shouting stirred her from her bed. An orange glow flickered outside her window. She looked to see men and women with poles desperately yanking burning thatch from the roofs. The whole row across the street was on fire.

Fortunately, rain came some hours later and extinguished the flames. But when she ventured down the alley in the misty morning air, the old woman's shop had been burnt to the ground, and all her trinkets were gone.

The fox pendant was nowhere to be found.

She went to the library and read about memory magic. When she left, she knew her moonblade had another throat to cut.

A WITCH STOPS

There was a time before Gilgara.

There was a time before Durmedia.

Before the Samerens left their hunting grounds.

Before the dwarves came from the east to settle the mountains.

Before they knew the power of moongems.

An age governed by might and terror, when giants and trolls scrapped over rivers and mountains and people were whipped to the brink.

Before the giants lost their memories, before the trolls were driven into the barren peaks.

They made humanity a beast of burden.

Their bodies tossed aside like toothpicks once they'd served their purpose, to have shamans wedge moongems between their ribs to give them life again.

Those men and women still haunted the deep places, the yawning caves and primordial ruins buried in slick mud and snaking roots, lost in the core of the earth.

It was a time before memory, before justice and record.

But they endured.

And they remembered.

And they built a race of grey men who would remember such things, so no injustice might be forgotten again.

So the world might remember, and learn from ages past.

The witch stared into the flames as the memories rolled past her eyes. She crushed a handful of berries in her palm, the viscous jelly oozing between her fingers as her face flushed with anger.

That was the role of a Keeper.

The one who had betrayed the Concordat of Memory would die.

THE KING OF VOLEREN

Talfrin swept his blue-and-white-checked cloak over his shoulder, showering the stable floor with snow. He patted Spens's mane. 'You rode well,' he said, wondering if he'd see the beast again. He glanced at the tumbledown inn, the wooden sign eaten by rot. Such inns, lying along less-travelled roads in the middle of the forest, often harboured the most desperate people. They would think nothing of stealing a horse in the night—even a thin, knobbly one like Spens.

A whinny made him turn around. In the opposite stable were two beautiful palfreys, one black and one white, their breath fogging the evening air.

He took a step back, letting out a small gasp.

They would be worth a fortune.

Bandits, then, he concluded. There was no way they'd have been brought here by choice. Someone must have stolen them – taken them from some noble's carriage train, most likely.

He crossed the courtyard, the cold seeping through his boots.

The inn was warm, though not much else good could be said about it. The main room reeked of urine, and the few patrons still awake at this hour were slumped in dark corners, their tongues lolling from their mouths. All except two.

With their crisp, bold-coloured clothes and neat beards, they stood out from the rest almost comically. And the way they balanced on their toes on their stools, lifting their behinds off the seats, told Talfrin they weren't used to staying in places like this.

The lighter-haired of the two, with bright blue eyes, gestured to Talfrin as he entered. 'Ah, here's someone now,' he said. 'Perhaps he knows?'

'What might I know?' Talfrin asked.

'The quickest way out of this wretched hole,' the darker-haired one grumbled.

Talfrin caught the sad stare of the barkeep, a small man with a wiry, unkempt beard.

'What Rils meant to ask,' the other said, 'is do you know the way to Volur City from here?'

Talfrin nodded, saying nothing.

'Finally, some luck. My name is Wayec, and this is Rilsan. We're on our way to Volur City to make a trade, though we lost our way somehow.'

'Unusual for a merchant to lose their way,' Talfrin said. 'You're either cheap and bought a bad map, thick as horseshit, or you're lying. Which is it?'

Both men stared at him with open mouths.

'I won't work with him,' Rilsan said, turning away.

'We need him,' Wayec said.

'Too bad. We can wait for the next.'

'How many others do you think there'll be?' Wayec said.

Rilsan sighed. Eventually, he shrugged. 'Fine.'

'There was a storm, to answer your question,' Wayec said, though he wasn't smiling any more. 'Near enough drowned us. We followed the road, must have missed a crossing. Stopped at the first light we saw, and that brought us here.'

'Must have gone a long way off,' Talfrin said with a shrug. 'No crossings for miles, the way you came.'

'You want the job or not?' Rilsan snarled. 'We pay well. Pay even better if you keep your mouth shut.'

'I don't need money.'

'He said nothing about money,' Wayec said with a knowing look.

Talfrin played with the hem of his shirt, weighing the men up. Volur City would take him the wrong way. He always hated to back out of a contract.

'I'm not looking for sex, if that's what you're getting at,' Talfrin said.

Wayec was undeterred. He offered his hand. 'I'm sure you know what I mean.'

There was something in the way Wayec looked at him that made him pause.

'I have a job already.'

'Oh,' the merchant said. 'What is it?'

'Got a village to protect from some sprakes. Easy pay, and the promise of particularly interesting treasure.'

Wayec's eyes glinted. Talfrin saw the impression of a deep, cold intelligence behind them, a mind totally opposite to his friendly demeanour. 'Particularly interesting treasure? I'm sure we could match that.'

'For escorting you to Volur City?'

'Indeed,' Wayec said with a disarming smile. 'Easiest treasure you'll ever earn.'

Somehow, he doubted that.

Talfrin cursed his luck. Even here, as far west as west could go, complications haunted him.

But there was something about these two travellers that told him they were more than mere merchants.

'What kind of treasure?'

Rilsan spoke up. 'Conventionally shiny. Haunts your dreams. Dangerous stuff, for sure.'

That piqued Talfrin's interest.

Wayec offered his hand. 'Will you be our escort?'

Talfrin took the hand. 'To Volur City.'

He smiled. 'We leave tomorrow, before breakfast.'

***

Talfrin emerged in the wintry dawn air, rolling his joints and stretching. It was a crisp day, and his muscles already hurt from days on the road. He didn't want to risk an injury.

The morning was quiet as he made his way across the courtyard to the stable. He smiled when Spens picked himself up off the floor and whinnied over the stable door.

'You made it,' Talfrin said.

As he was watering Spens, the cawing of a crow broke the silent morning. Vicious cawing, an intruder call, the kind they use when another bird strays too close to their nest. He turned to see the lone bird perched on the gabled roof of an outbuilding, shoulders hunched, beak aimed straight at the inn door.

The merchants were making their way down the courtyard, Rilsan rubbing his hands together for warmth.

'Morning,' Wayec called out.

'You've upset the bird,' Talfrin said.

'So we have.' Wayec couldn't have looked less interested, and he ignored the bird entirely as it continued to squawk.

They saddled up and headed off, trundling down the dirt road at a steady pace. Talfrin dipped into his pack of nuts and dried berries and nibbled as he watched the sky for the crow.

Unusual behaviour for a bird.

'We have a lengthy ride ahead of us,' Wayec said. 'This road gets worse before it gets better.'

'I thought you'd never been this way?'

'I've travelled this way hundreds of times. We don't want you for your navigation skills, Bladekin.'

It was the first time they'd addressed his profession. 'What do you want me for, then?'

'We couldn't speak of it in the inn,' Rilsan said gruffly. 'Never know who's listening. The king of Voleren is dead.'

The news caught Talfrin by surprise. Roltast, the young, cunning king of Voleren. The last time Talfrin met him, they discussed the work of Bladekin in his kingdom. Though his reign had come at a dark time, and his policies caused some hardship, Talfrin believed he genuinely cared for his people.

And what was more, a powerful magic protected him.

Only powerful sorcery could have broken such a shield.

'Roltast?' Talfrin asked. He left out the king's title on purpose.

'*King* Roltast,' Wayec corrected immediately.

Royal agents, then.

'Yes, dead,' Wayec continued. 'By the hand of some magic weapon, it seems.'

'How do you know?'

'His wounds were jagged, no sign of healing. Only a magic blade could have inflicted such an injury. He was protected by magical means.'

'You suspect an assassination?'

'He certainly didn't do it himself,' Rilsan said.

'We do,' Wayec said. 'And we'd like you to see if you can identify the weapon, and help us find it.'

'I don't get involved with royalty.'

'Too late,' Rilsan said.

Talfrin was quiet for a while. 'It will take some exceptionally interesting treasure to sway me. What's the payment?'

'Naturally, if we find the offending weapon, you're free to take it. It would serve us all good to have that blade gone. As a token of good faith, though, I have this.'

Wayec pulled out a chain from behind his tunic, revealing a pendant. It was a bright, untarnished silver. The face of a fox sneered at him, following his movements with orange gemstone eyes.

He felt the pull of it immediately.

'Where did you get that?'

'A fellow in a market. He was wailing about wanting to get rid of it. I could feel its magic.'

'And you thought you could bribe a Bladekin into interfering in politics with it?'

'Think of it, you'd be doing the world a service. Removing two dangerous magical objects and restoring order to a kingdom. That's within your code, surely?'

Talfrin said nothing. They knew it was pushing the boundaries. But strictly, finding the sword would be allowed under the Bladekin code. 'What will you do with the owner of the blade?'

Rilsan grinned. 'Give them a slap on the head and tell them not to do it again.'

Wayec spoke up. 'If you don't help, who knows how much harm they could do?'

'Not much,' Talfrin said. 'People who strike kings don't tend to strike again.'

'You don't know that.'

He sighed. 'I'll go to Volur City, look at your king. You'll give me the pendant. I'll tell you what I learn from the wounds. We'll see how dangerous the weapon is before we go further. How does that sound?'

Wayec didn't respond for a while. 'Fine,' he said, with no hint of mirth in his voice.

As the word left his lips, the crow cawed again. It circled above them, coming to rest on a spiny tree far ahead, and watched as they rode.

***

It had been a long time since Talfrin had seen Volur City.

Truthfully, he liked to spend as little time there as possible. Voleren was a strange kingdom, full of wizards and scholars. Magic was stronger here than elsewhere in the world. Some said it was because there were large moongem deposits in the northern mountains, a place the dwarves had never been.

Talfrin didn't care. But it was a place that made him uncomfortable.

They rode through the vaulted gates of the city walls, the high parapets bearing the stone faces of many animals. A lion seemed to snarl at him, its face frozen.

'Straight to the palace,' Talfrin said. 'I don't mean to spend the night here.'

Wayec grimaced. 'Is our city so offensive?'

Talfrin said nothing. The street was clean, paved with large white stones. The fronts of the houses were immaculate, many of the windows unshuttered. Clearly, they weren't afraid of night thieves.

But a Bladekin had a sense for magic, and here, it prickled his skin like a cold wind.

The prickle grew as they approached the palace.

King Roltast's body lay in a dim room set high in the roofbeams of the palace. Talfrin shook off the exhaustion of climbing several flights of stairs and lifted the corner of the silken veil.

'Careful,' Wayec said.

Talfrin glared. 'You want to know or not?'

The agent backed away. 'Just be gentle with him.'

He removed the veil, letting it drop to the floor. There was a rough gash down the king's side, the pale flesh ripped and open, with a texture like parchment.

He knew the mark immediately.

'A moonblade,' he said.

'What's a moonblade?'

A brutal weapon. Ancient, their origins not understood by many – including Talfrin. He left that to the scholars back at Kadahrn.

He knew the important things.

'A deep wound from a moonblade cannot be healed, not least by any known means. They are an excellent weapon for an assassin.'

Wayec paled. He shared a glance with Rilsan, who turned away.

'An assassin will be hard to track,' Talfrin said. 'Practically impossible. They've killed their target, and they don't usually stick around. Could be anywhere.'

Rilsan was pacing the room like a caged lion, while Wayec watched on. There was a strange look in his eyes.

Talfrin rolled his shoulders. 'Well, I've done what I said I would. I've told you what you need to do.'

'Wait,' Wayec said. 'We've no way of finding it without you.'

Talfrin shrugged. 'I've no idea where they've taken it. I'm as much use to you now as a dormouse.'

But Rilsan was looking at him. 'We might know how to find it. But it may take time.'

'Time?'

'Yes. And we'll need you nearby.'

'I'm not staying in this city.'

'With respect,' Rilsan said, 'I don't see that you have much of a choice. That is, if you want to remain a friend of Voleren.'

Talfrin clenched his fists, but he forced down his anger. 'How long?'

'A few days.'

'You have a suspect?'

Rilsan gave him a nasty smile. 'More than a suspect.'

***

Talfrin shoved the door of the inn open.

He doubted the men, and he disliked their secrecy.

And he disliked having to spend a night in Volur City.

The common room was, unsurprisingly, immaculate, every table polished and every chair cushion bright and clean. The chatter was polite, and several eyes turned to look at this scruffy, road-weary traveller, with his patchy blue and white cloak and a streak of grey in his black hair, which splayed around his shoulders.

They averted their eyes when they saw the Bladekin tattoo on his cheek.

He ordered the smallest room and vanished upstairs without another word.

Sitting beside the compact fireplace of his private room, he cradled the pendant in his hand. *Where might they have found it?*

The silver glistened in the fire's light, reflecting the flames. The orange stones were pure and bright, the fox crafted with great skill. The men said they got it from a trader, but Talfrin wondered if there was something more at work.

There was a potent magic in it.

Tucking it back in his pocket, he unfolded the contract he'd originally come out here to do and studied it.

Protecting a small lumber village from a tribe of sprakes. Easy, simple money. And no politics.

Why had he stopped to speak to them? He should have known they were trouble. There was a glint in their eyes, a hardness. He knew they weren't merchants the second he saw them.

But he'd always been curious. And that wasn't something he regretted.

He folded the contract up and threw it into the fire.

His eyes closed. There was nothing else for it now.

He would see where this took him.

***

The air bit his flesh. When he looked down, his blue and white cloak was missing. Instead, all he wore were ripped rags.

He clutched his shoulders for warmth. The night was black, the street empty. The streetlamps no longer burned.

But there was a glow on the horizon.

He climbed a sloped street, hoping to get a better view.

In the distance, he saw flames shooting from a castle's windows and roofs. They drank the night air like water, casting an orange stain across the sky. He saw a banner frantically flapping in the wind. On it, a grinning moon seemed to scream.

By his feet, a fox watched.

The fire spread across the city, and he fled in vain as it ate the buildings surrounding him.

***

When he woke, he could hardly move his upper body.

A few tender presses with his fingers told him he'd been tense last night, and now his neck and shoulders were paying for it. He did some tentative stretches, rolled his shoulders and gently massaged his skin.

Usually, he didn't remember his dreams. But he remembered that one.

He pulled out the pendant again and cupped it in his hands. It was warm to the touch.

Locking eyes with the fox, it was as though he were looking at a living thing.

The scholars at Kadahrn had spoken of such magic before. Where people impress their images onto objects, imbuing them with their strongest memories. It was an extremely powerful kind of magic, to project those images onto someone else's thoughts. Few were capable of it.

Already, he was beginning to recognise the echoes of somebody else in him. A feeling of connection to this castle he saw, an anger at the grinning moon and a sense of deep injustice. And rage. A pure, all-consuming rage.

***

The rage burned in his stomach like hot coals as he made his way to the palace. The soldiers admitted him without asking. They were used to his face now.

As he had done every day since arriving, he asked to see Wayec and waited in the throne room. Inevitably, Wayec would send a messenger down to tell him they were still working on it, and Talfrin would send an angry message back and stalk away.

This time was different.

'Bladekin?'

The woman who spoke was round and soft-featured, her belly bulging against the cloud-blue tabard that all officials in Volur City wore. Her silver hair was tied back in a ponytail.

'That's me. Is Wayec ever coming down to see me, or is he going to keep cowering behind royal clerks?'

The woman offered a small smile. 'I'm not here to talk about Wayec.'

'Then why are you wasting my time?'

That smile remained on her thin lips, knowing, unreadable. 'Come with me.'

He was instantly suspicious. With an assassin around, it was not the time to be disappearing into lonely corridors with strangers.

But she was persistent. 'You possess a certain trinket. A silver necklace, bearing the features of a fox.'

He instinctively pushed it deeper into his pocket.

'I would speak to you about it, but we must be alone.'

With that she turned and walked away.

Every instinct told him not to follow her.

But he was always too curious.

She led him down winding corridors and several flights of stone stairs. Before long, there were no more windows and she had to light the way with a lantern. They went through a heavy wooden door and its hinges groaned from years of disuse. They were in a dingy storage room stacked full of barrels. Dust tickled his nose.

She leant in and whispered as though someone might overhear them. 'The Moonblade Princess wants to meet with you.'

***

The next day, Wayec sent a messenger to Talfrin, asking him to come to the palace that night.

As night fell, he threw on his blue and white cloak and stepped out into the cold, his nose buried in his shirt for warmth.

He walked away from the palace.

The Moonblade Princess had chosen a secluded place for their meeting. He'd already been to scout it out during the day, but he was still nervous. His reflexes weren't as quick as they once were, and the moonblade made him wary. Though it had served its purpose, he doubted she'd give it up easily.

But that was what his blade was for.

He'd taken to wearing the pendant around his neck. It radiated a warmth which was comforting in the night cold, and the faint anger it gave him helped soothe his fear.

The meeting place was a crooked alleyway between two rows of old, dilapidated terraces, half of which looked abandoned. The muddy ground squelched around his boots, making a subtle approach all but impossible.

She was cunning.

He stopped halfway down the alley and leant against the wall, lingering in a shadow and waiting for her to appear.

He needn't have bothered.

'I wondered if you'd come,' said a light voice.

He looked up to see a hooded figure leaning over a balcony. She vaulted onto the bannister, gathered herself and somersaulted down to the alley floor, bending her legs as she hit to absorb the shock.

'Impressed you didn't slip over.'

'I had to choose a place you couldn't sneak up on me,' she said. She flicked her cloak aside, placing a hand on the hilt of the moonblade.

His eyes lingered on it a little too long.

She smirked. 'Just in case you decided to kill me and take the blade.'

'Who says I won't do that, regardless?'

'I think you're too smart for that. I have a deadly weapon, and you don't know my abilities. You'll want to observe me first, at least to learn any potential weaknesses you can take advantage of.' She drew the sword. The blade shined in the dark, a gentle, milky white. It lit up her face.

A sharp jawline, wide cheekbones and green, calculating eyes. Pale skin.

'Very smart,' he said. 'Why did you kill him?'

The sudden question seemed to catch her off guard. 'Roltast? He was a bad king.'

'I've seen bad kings. Trust me, if he was evil, you'd have known.'

Her nostrils flared. 'I knew. I saw the suffering of his people firsthand. It never happened in our father's reign.'

'And you saw the need to take matters into your own hands?'

Her eyes were green fires. 'If those with the ability to act do nothing, what hope is there for those who can't? It was my duty to protect them.'

He smiled. 'Your duty is done, then. You can hand me the blade.'

She backed off, watching him carefully. 'I'm not finished with it yet. Tell me, Bladekin. How familiar are you with the city of Thrynn?'

'I've been there once or twice.'

She tilted her head, as though analysing him. He resisted the urge to touch the pendant.

'And its history? What do you know of that?'

'It's the main port of Guenteria. Has been for centuries. It's an old place, much of it has slipped into the sea over the years. Lord Bedivar is its ruler.' He remembered his dream. 'The lord of the grinning moon.'

'Indeed,' she said, nodding. 'Not a land touched by the Keepers, either. It wasn't Old Durmedian.'

He nodded.

'Bedivar's family have been lords for generations. Do you know who came before?'

'It's an old tale,' he said with a sweep of his hand. 'The lord who perished in a fire. A story for children.'

'Not just a story,' the Moonblade Princess said, and the corner of her mouth curled into a smile. It was the smile of a hunter. 'That old lord was real.'

'What of it?'

'His sigil was the fox, his animal the crow.'

He thought of the crow that followed them up the road, and the fox he saw in his dream.

It's just an enchantment. An echo of an echo. Nothing more.

'You're distracting me with talk of ghosts. I'm here for that sword. Offer me a deal, or we have nothing to talk about.'

His hand moved to his sword.

As fast as he could blink, she jabbed the moonblade towards him, angling the point at his chest.

'That pendant you wear.'

'You can't have it,' he said immediately.

She laughed. 'I don't want it. Nobody wants that curse on them.'

'Curse?'

'I've held it. I know what it does to you.'

He said nothing.

She continued. 'Bad dreams. A city on fire, and a fox.'

'I intend to destroy it.'

'Oh, no doubt,' she said with a smile. 'But you know the nature of it, don't you?'

'It holds an impression. A capsule of someone's old thoughts. Not uncommon.'

'Not old,' she said. 'Those thoughts are alive.' She whispered her next words. 'There's memory magic at play here.'

He clenched his teeth. 'What does it matter? The lord is long dead. I have the strength in me to destroy it. And that blade, too. The type of magic is irrelevant. Hand it to me.'

She took two steps back. 'No. I still have need of it.'

'What for?'

'I believe the old lord is still alive.'

Talfrin scoffed. 'Conspiracy now, is it?'

'More than conspiracy. Have you seen the crows?'

He said nothing, but he heard the cawing of the crow at the inn. The fiery burn of its eye was seared onto his memory.

'A crow appeared before two merchants in Thrynn,' she continued, 'the day before their shops burned down. And the same thing happened to me on the Old West Road. That was where I first saw it, in an old pawn shop in a dingy alley. The next morning, the shop was burnt and the pendant was gone.'

Talfrin frowned. 'It would take some powerful magic to have that control. And to have survived all these years.'

'He may have support,' she said. 'There's a story about a woman who passed through Thrynn. Someone tried to recruit her, said he worked for the fox. When she refused, they burned the inn down. If the lord is still alive, it seems he's using powerful magic. Memory magic. We both know very few people wield that skill.' Her green eyes seemed to see right through him. 'A Keeper.'

He shook his head. 'You're asking me to believe something impossible, and all you have to back it up are shadows and maybes.'

'Impossible? For a Keeper to go rogue? They are as human as you or I, and just as fallible.'

'They aren't the same. Keepers are bound. They can't use their powers for themselves.'

'What if you're wrong?'

He had no answer to that. The night sounds of the city filled the gap; the odd shout, the clatter of doors and windows being shuttered.

'Only a moonblade would be certain to kill him,' the princess said. 'I thought the Bladekin's duty was to protect people.'

'Our duty is to remove magic from the hands of the public.'

'Yes. To prevent harm. Yet faced with a powerful sorcerer with a penchant for arson, you say you're not interested.'

'It's outside my scope.'

'Then you shan't have the blade,' she said and moved back.

He scowled. 'What makes you so eager to protect Thrynn? It's not your land.'

'This is all of our land. A threat anywhere is a threat everywhere. And I know enough about magic to see that something different is happening here.'

He stepped forward, drawing his blade as he went and sweeping it up under her, hoping to end this before it began. She was quick, though, and writhed aside, leaving his sword to hiss through the air.

She lashed out with her foot, slamming into the side of his calf and sending him tumbling to a knee.

He spun with a hasty slice, tearing through her cloak and part of her loose tunic, exposing the bare flesh of her arm.

But she moved out of range, and putting pressure on his leg sent waves of pain through his knee. She'd jarred it, if not worse. His footwork was ruined.

She remained at a distance, eyes on him. 'You'll recover in a few days,' she said. 'Give up the hunt. Let me go to Thrynn.'

'No chance.'

'Then you've failed your duty.' She disappeared down the alley.

The rage boiled in him.

***

Talfrin limped to the palace on a chilly day; snow swirled through the streets of Volur City and piled up against the whitewashed housefronts.

'Morning, Bladekin,' the soldier said and dipped his head as he passed. He recognised the man now, a youth who often ended up on the front gate. Sometimes he smiled, but today, Talfrin ignored him.

A dream played on his mind. A dream full of fire and screams, which echoed long after waking.

'How courteous of you to finally answer our summons,' Wayec said as he entered the office.

Talfrin shook snowflakes onto the patterned carpet. 'I'm not summoned anywhere. I go where I please.'

'So it would seem,' the agent said. His ice-blue eyes betrayed no emotion. 'Well, I have word for you.'

'You know where the assassin is?'

'I believe I do,' he said. 'Come with me.'

They passed through the main hall where courtiers bustled back and forth, all wearing the cloud blue royal garb. Some were elderly men and women with short hair and spectacles, ambling, their arms full of books and papers. The youths were the same, only they walked much quicker. A pair of serving staff hurried past clutching buckets and mops, while wealthy nobles paced in groups, conversing. Some laughed, but most had pursed lips and hard eyes. It was a dark time for their kingdom, after all.

King Roltast had left no heir, and the only other living member of their family, his sister, disappeared shortly after his reign began. If rumours were to be believed, the king hadn't left his bedchambers for three days after. Though they'd grown apart in adulthood, apparently their bonds were still deep.

He scanned the faces of the hall.

And stopped in his tracks.

The Moonblade Princess.

He was sure he'd seen her. That sharp jaw, those intelligent eyes, looking right at him.

But he saw no sign of her now. And it had been dark the night they met; she'd had her hood up. He hadn't got a proper look at her.

Perhaps he was mistaken.

'Keep up,' Wayec said. Talfrin followed.

They emerged in a high-roofed study full of dusty books. The bookshelves were secured behind meshed doors, so only those with the keys could access them.

Wayec sat in a cushioned chair. Talfrin took one opposite.

'We have eyes everywhere,' Wayec said. 'Not much escapes the sight of the king's servants.'

Talfrin wondered where they'd been on the night of the assassination, but said nothing.

'So when an assassin sneaks into the palace and kills the king, it doesn't go unnoticed.'

'I should imagine not,' Talfrin said.

Wayec ignored him. 'Fortunately for you, we have reason to believe this was an inside job. Someone opened the gates for them. She's been found now, found and tortured.'

Behind Wayec, a woman stood on a book ladder, sorting through some shelves. Talfrin noticed her muscles tense up at those words. She glanced around. Talfrin saw the Moonblade Princess looking at him.

Wayec frowned, turning to follow Talfrin's gaze.

'What did you learn?' Talfrin said, dragging the conversation back.

'She was one of Princess Nadina's most trusted staff before she disappeared,' Wayec said, turning back. 'Princess Nadina is still alive, and she orchestrated the plot.'

Talfrin knew she was within earshot. 'I suppose that makes her queen now, then?'

Wayec grimaced. 'Regicide and fratricide tend to disqualify people from holding power.'

'So what will you do? With no rightful heir?'

'That's not your problem, nor your place to ask, frankly, mercenary,' Wayec said. His friendly mask had slipped now, laying bare the cold, merciless politician behind it.

'Keep talking like that, I might not be so interested in your contract.'

'You will be. We'll pay you handsomely, and you don't have far to go. She's still in the city.'

'Oh?' he said, fighting not to look at the shelves again.

'She's waiting to meet with somebody. Apparently, she's travelling to Thrynn tomorrow. Lord Bedivar shall be warned.'

'Did this servant tell you who she was meeting with?'

Again, his cold eyes betrayed nothing. 'No.'

'So you have no idea?'

'Possibly another one of her accomplices,' Wayec said, not looking away. 'Remains to be seen. But we do know where she is staying: the Onyx Swan. Head there tonight and ask the barkeep for the royal room. He'll know what you mean.'

'I'm deep in politics now. I'm going to need compensation.'

Wayec offered a tight smile. 'I thought as much. Here, a hundred Voleri lions; that should be more than enough.'

Talfrin weighed the coinpurse before pocketing it.

'A long reign to you,' he said with a bow.

Wayec smiled again.

As Talfrin made his way back through the streets, the dream filled his mind once more. A whole city burning, a flock of crows soaring ahead. A fox ready to strike.

***

The flames licked around the blackened log like hungry wolves on a felled ox. The log burned slowly, cracking and turning white. When it was little more than ash, a serving boy entered and threw some fresh, dry wood into the fireplace. The fire crackled gleefully and feasted.

And still Talfrin had no answer.

It had been too long since he finished his studies at Kadahrn. The minutiae of the Bladekin code eluded him.

He'd failed to defeat her. And while he thought she'd only struck out of a desire to help, it played on his mind. He couldn't allow someone to walk away with something as dangerous as a moonblade.

Which made Wayec's offer very tempting.

And yet, damn him, Talfrin would struggle to do it. He sympathised with her. That desire to use magic for good. Though arguably she'd already made things worse by plunging Voleren into a succession crisis.

This was why it had to be taken from her.

Who knew what chaos she could wreak in Thrynn, if any part of her suspicion was false? It was a strong case, but not foolproof. Fires, this fox, whispers of an ancient lord. It could be something.

Or it could be some pretender, an excited peasant weaving a narrative to seize power for themselves. Such things weren't unheard of.

And if a moonblade was unleashed on a city like that – if she somehow lost it – there was no telling what harm could be done.

He sat and stared as the new firewood slowly sank into the flames, the fire's heat increasing.

The code seemed to show a path forward.

She would have to relinquish the blade, one way or another. That was the imminent threat. He would destroy it.

He would go to Thrynn after, explore on his own. He was reluctant, but her case was strong.

And the pendant called him there.

'*To Thrynn. Destroy the blade, and come to Thrynn.*'
Were they his thoughts, or the words of someone else?

***

A witch with straight white hair and a scar at the right corner of her mouth passed below a stone lion frozen in a snarl, and entered Volur City.

The moon was high in the sky, and the door of the inn was locked. She released the latch with a flick of her hand, forcing the tumblers to remember the last time they felt the touch of a key.

An innocent piece of memory magic.

The hall was black and deserted. She crept towards the stairs, but froze when she heard rustling behind the counter.

Slowly, she drew the moongem from her pouch, the glow casting the hall in a ghostly light.

'Who's there?' she whispered.

A rat scurried across the floorboards, observed her for a second, and disappeared into the gloom. The room fell silent.

She smiled.

She found the Bladekin asleep beside his fire, which had long burnt out. Even in sleep he looked troubled; his eyes were closed too tightly, his forehead creased by a frown.

'Talfrin the Bladekin,' she whispered.

He stirred. His dark eyes came to rest on hers, devoid of surprise. She saw a kindness behind them, though he disguised it well.

'What do you want?'

She saw his hand shift to his blade beneath his cloak – barely perceptible, but then, she never missed a thing like that.

'I'm not here to harm you, so you have no need for that blade.' She smiled. 'I come to you with a message.'

He rubbed his face. 'Seems all I get these days are messages. I'm very busy.'

'It's an important message.'

'From who?'

'From a tomb beneath a glittering lake in the far north.'

The Bladekin's eyes widened. He was silent for a moment, hunting for words.

'A witch brings word from a Keeper's shrine.'

She nodded.

He must have read her expression, because his face was forlorn. 'What is it?'

'It is simple, but hard to hear. There is a rogue Keeper in Thrynn.'

Colour drained from Talfrin's face. He sat for a long while, head resting on his hand. She detected a slight tremble in his shoulders. 'How?'

'That is a matter for another time. I, the Keepers and the scholars at Kadahrn will discuss it when all this is over. For now, we need you to act.'

'You're asking me to break the oldest code.' There was anger in his eyes. 'Never should a Bladekin and a Keeper cross blades. Never.'

'This one is a Keeper no more.'

He clenched his teeth and stared out the window. Below, Volur City had fallen into silence. Raindrops speckled the glass, racing to the bottom. Their dull thudding was the only sound.

'Why me?'

'You're the only one who'll do this.'

'The rest of my kin said no?'

'They did.'

'And what makes you think I'll say yes?'

'I've seen you, Talfrin. You care about the people. More than your code. Besides, you're too curious.'

He frowned. 'And what about the moonblade? Am I supposed to let her go?'

'You decide what to do with her.' The witch shrugged. 'What does it matter? A stray moonblade does not compare to the damage Lovican could cause, should he succeed. Kill her and take the blade, if you must. I believe you have an assignment. And you could use it if you're going to face him.'

'I don't like my odds,' he said. There was a melancholy in his face; his cheeks already seemed shallower. 'I haven't seen Thrynn in a long time.'

'You need not act alone,' she said, and reached into her pouch. She handed a cold bottle to him. It was dark green and rounded at the neck, stoppered with a cork and bound with string. A thin, dark liquid sloshed within.

He took it with a frown. 'What is this?'

'You will find the Keeper's bark is worse than his bite,' she said. 'This should silence the barking. But only drink it at the last moment. Do you hear? The last moment.'

***

The Onyx Swan was a pretty inn. Spotless, like most of Volur City, with a black tiled roof and mottled walls.

He asked for the royal room.

The inn was quiet and largely empty, most patrons having either left or gone to bed. He crept up three flights of stairs, collecting himself before knocking on her door.

His hand rested on the pommel of his blade.

The heavy door opened, and two green eyes stared at him from above the point of the glowing sword.

'I'm not here to hurt you.'

'I heard your conversation,' she said. 'You know who I am now. What a catch, a royal princess.'

'It actually makes you less of a target. I don't like to get involved with royalty.'

'Then why are you even doing this?'

'Curiosity got the better of me.' He shrugged. 'If I'd have wanted to betray you, I'd have told Wayec when I saw you in the palace.'

A slight smile appeared on her pursed pink lips. The sword point lowered a fraction. 'What brought you here?'

He smiled. 'Curiosity.'

'Curiosity?' The corner of her mouth flickered.

'I've decided. We should go to Thrynn.'

'Wait. We?'

'Us. Together.'

She narrowed her eyes. 'Why?'

'You beat me in one-on-one combat, and my foot is ruined, thanks to you. I'm going to need someone with me. Someone who knows how to wield that blade.'

'What if Wayec comes after us?'

'I don't think he will.'

'But if he does?' Suddenly, he saw the weight of the last few months on her shoulders, the paranoia that follows an assassin like a cloud, never lifting. There was desperation in her eyes.

'Then we'll face him together.'

After a moment, she stepped aside, letting him in. He sat on the edge of the bed. Like everything else in Volur City, it was exceptionally clean.

THE KEEPER

They arrived in Thrynn after dark.

After passing through the gate, Nadina headed down the main street, a vein that led straight to the market square.

Talfrin watched her walk. The Moonblade Princess, her slight frame buried beneath layers of black. She paused outside one inn, listening to the voices within, before moving on.

With luck, she'd find a quiet place for them. With two beds.

Talfrin ducked into a side street, heading towards the docks and the stinking slums that spilled down to the green, opaque waters of the bay. He had a meeting to attend.

The silence of the streets unnerved him. He kept his weapon close. The last time he came to Thrynn, it was not unusual to see folks loitering, even after dark. But now the close alleys were deserted, the windows shuttered and silent. Even the doors to the inns remained closed, their thresholds clear of the drunks and old men who usually watched the nightwalkers pass. Candlelight flickered within, though, telling him some people still lived in Thrynn after all.

He followed the trail through the snaking maze of hovels, glancing at the rough map he clutched. Portside was a place he'd visited many times, but always skirting the edge on his way to the docks itself. He'd never ventured so far within the tangle of driftwood and stagnant pools. Every ramshackle home was pressed up against its neighbour, leaning on it for support. Not a bug could have squeezed between them.

Until he came to a gap.

Around a small lake, the street of mangled cobbles suddenly opened up. Against its right side wasn't a row of houses, but a charred black strip of land. Nothing remained besides the odd piece of burnt wood jutting upwards, looking like the tangled remains of the ships they'd passed on their journey, half-sank along the coast, their pilots having missed the beacon.

Standing beside this wreck was a woman holding a lantern; there was a cowl over her head to keep off the night rain.

'Axi?' he asked.

'Talfrin,' she replied. She met his eyes, unperturbed by his Bladekin tattoo. The instant challenge in her face told him she was used to confrontation. 'I was beginning to think you weren't coming.'

'Lost my way,' he said. 'The streets are darker than I remember.'

'Folks are scared.' She gestured to the charred ruin. 'They don't want to be next.'

He paced slowly along the edge of the street, studying the remains. He made out the remnants of the occasional piece of furniture. Stone hearths still stood in places, covered in ash. But there was very little to be learned from them. Nearly everything had been destroyed. 'You think there will be more attacks?'

'There have been several already,' she said. 'Always targeted. Why not more? The Fox seems to delight in terror.'

The Fox. He thought back on the dreams, which had only turned more violent on their journey south. He glanced up the empty street. 'I'm surprised there aren't any wardens out.'

'They're scared, too,' she said with a shrug. 'Bedivar is many things, but intimidating isn't one of them. Faced with the prospect of encountering a fire spectre in the night, most choose to stay in the guard tower and drink all night. They fear the streets more than their lord.'

'Fiery spectres?'

'So the stories say,' she said with a grimace.

'You don't believe them.'

'I was in this inn the night it burned,' she said. 'Though I didn't see the fire start. Others who have seen these fires say they've spied fiery spirits walking the street in the hours before. I don't think so.'

'What makes you say that?'

'The night the inn burned, a man approached me. Told me he needed warriors. I was… less than polite. That night, the inn was torched. I suspect that was more than mere coincidence.'

'Did you know the man?'

She stared for a while at the burned ruin. 'I had a dream that night. Lord Lovican was in it. I seemed to think he was the same man, but honestly, I can't remember his face. And dreams are fickle.'

They came to the ruin of the inn. It had a bigger foundation than the buildings either side, and three stone steps leading up to what would have been the door, but he wouldn't have recognised it if Axi hadn't pointed it out.

He crossed the threshold and scanned the floor, moving rubble aside. Within seconds, his hands were black.

'So you didn't see the fire start?'

'No. When I woke, I was standing in the street, shivering. I must have sleep-walked away.'

'And you dreamt of the old lord?'

She nodded.

'Have your dreamt of him before?'

'No. My dream felt like a recollection, though. As though I had met him before. He saved me. He seemed affectionate.'

'Perhaps he pushed that dream onto you. Perhaps he wanted to save you from the fire.'

'If he wanted to save me, he wouldn't have set the fire in the first place. Besides, the affection was just for show. For the crowds. I saw the malice in his eyes, even in the dream.'

Usually, Talfrin would have dismissed such talk of dreams out of hand. He usually believed they were nothing but the echoes of a restless mind.

But these dreams were different.

Talfrin wiped his hands on his breeches. Nothing in the main hall. He moved on, following the phantom outline of the building's foundations.

'What did the stranger say to you in the inn?'

'He told me the Fox watches, and that he was the rightful lord of the city. He was recruiting soldiers.'

'Do you think he was recruiting you?'

'I believe so. He knew my name.'

Talfrin said nothing, but continued to dig through the rubble. Occasional scraps of metal appeared, which had somehow survived the intense flames – the reinforced corners of crates, barrel hoops, and candelabras.

There was nothing left. Even if the innkeep had survived, the business was ruined. As were the homes and lives of everyone who once lived on this street.

That seemed an extreme reaction to someone saying no.

The cold night dug its fingers into his flesh, the rain dripping from his hair. Before long, even Axi was shivering a little beneath her cloak and mail armour.

He was ready to give up. Shrugging his shoulders, he made his way back towards the door.

Beside the stone steps, he glimpsed something silver in the ash. Kicking the ash off, he saw it was a short blade.

The point was sharp, the edge kept in excellent condition. Ready to be used.

'Bring that lantern, please.'

In the light's glow, he could make out more detail. A patterned blade, but a simple hilt with no decoration. The pommel, though, was what made it most interesting.

A luscious red. On it, the shield-shaped badge of the University of Rostagam.

'Recognise this?' Talfrin said.

She shook her head. 'No, but not many Rostagam graduates here, to say the least. Might be worth checking with a fence. They might know the owner.'

He raised an eyebrow.

She shrugged. 'I wasn't always a noble mercenary.'

***

Axi left him at the door of an unassuming tavern, just off the main street.

'You're sure this is the place?'

She smiled. 'I'm sure. Ask for Zenya.'

The air within was dense and warm, and carried the lingering whiff of spilled beer. Still, the floorboards were bright and varnished and looked as though they were regularly mopped. The tables were clean and the cramped hall was full of people from all walks of life, not just the down-and-outs. It looked every bit like an average, respectable tavern.

Not the place you'd meet a fence.

Which meant the fence was good at their job.

He asked a young man carrying an armful of tankards if he could speak to Zenya. He barely batted an eye, but gestured towards a woman in the corner facing away from them.

'Zenya?' he said as he approached.

She turned slowly, her dark eyes locking straight on his. Fiery, confident, entirely feral.

'Come with me,' she said.

The dark backrooms of the inn were cluttered and dusty, full of burlap sacks and old barrels. He reckoned that if he cracked one of them open, he wouldn't find alcohol inside.

Zenya hopped up on a crate and crossed her legs, studying him.

'You have something for me.'

'How did you know?'

She gave him a smile, which made the hairs on his neck stand up. It was not a safe smile. 'Reading people is my job. And you're an open book.'

'Is that so?' He folded his arms. 'So what brings me here?'

'You're a Bladekin,' she said, 'so you won't want to sell me anything. You're probably looking for some enchanted item, and wondering if it's passed through my hands. I'll tell you right now, it hasn't.'

'Close,' he said. 'I'm not selling. But all I want from you is information.'

Her brows knotted in confusion for a moment. 'Alright, spill. I'll see what I can do.'

He pulled out the dagger.

Her mask slipped. Jaw tightened, eyes flicking from the blade to him. She recognised it. And she knew he'd noticed.

'I need to know who owns this dagger.'

'That stupid boy,' she whispered. 'What do you want with him?'

'I want to ask his opinion on something.'

She smiled wryly. 'Very funny. He's an idiot, but he's a close friend of mine. You hurt him, there's not a place in this world you'll be safe. But if you just want to talk, I can arrange that.'

He let the threat pass, though he felt the coals of anger stirring in his stomach, spurred by the pendant around his neck. Normally, he felt no need to defend his pride.

The magic in that piece of jewellery was strong indeed.

'I won't lay a finger on him.'

'Then wait here.'

Moments later, he was alone with the man. As thin as a rapier, his black hair was matted and tangled around his cheeks. His shoulders were hunched, his eyes low. Talfrin felt some pity for him.

He held out the dagger. 'This yours?'

'Yes.'

'You know where I found it, don't you?'

'Yes.'

Talfrin handed him the dagger and sat on the edge of a barrel, gesturing for the man to do the same.

'I'm going to ask you some questions. I want you to answer them truthfully. Alright?'

He nodded. His eyes were already shiny, ready to shed tears.

'What's your name?'

'Rafi.'

'Your trade?'

'I wait tables for Zennie.'

'Before that?'

He looked away. His leg bounced restlessly. 'Thief.'

'Don't worry, I don't hold that against you. Did you steal this dagger, too?'

'No,' he said immediately. 'No, I didn't. It was a reward for graduation.'

'A graduate turned thief. What happened?'

He shrugged. 'One bad thing after another. It's life.'

'Someone from such a responsible background would only turn to thievery if they had to for survival. Am I right, Rafi?'

Rafi nodded after a pause. His bottom lip trembled.

'And the pay here, it's not enough, is it?'

He shook his head.

Talfrin studied him. He could see it. If you trimmed his hair and shaved his beard, there was a studious man beneath it all. He was kind and thoughtful. He would have made an excellent clerk in the royal chancery. But such was the way of things.

'You don't seem the type to be setting fires for no reason.'

Rafi burst into tears at those words. Quiet sobs, suppressed by the back of his hand. 'I'm not. I swear.'

'But maybe the type who would do something stupid for the promise of coin.'

More sobs, but Rafi said nothing.

He pulled the pendant out from under his shirt. 'Do you recognise this sigil, Rafi?'

Rafi's eyes widened, his body tense. He stood up. 'Where did you get that?'

Talfrin frowned. 'Some merchants gave it to me. You've seen it before?'

Rafi grimaced. 'I stole the damn thing. Someone from out of the city sold it to a pawnbroker. I stole it. Then the shop burned.'

'Did it have an effect on you?'

'The dreams. You too?'

Talfrin nodded.

'Get rid of it as fast as you can. They'll only get worse. And he's looking for it.'

All pretence had fallen away. Talfrin knew exactly who he meant. And Rafi knew, too.

'If you know the sigil, you know the Fox. Lord Lovican. Is he the one you're setting fires for?'

Rafi nodded.

'Why?'

'I have no choice. He blamed me for the loss of the pendant. Said if I set the fires, he'd pay my – my rent,' he said between sobs. 'If not, he'd kill me.'

'Where can I find him?'

'I don't know. He always finds me.'

'Not an inkling? You're more wrapped up in this than anyone, you must know something.'

'If I had my way, I'd never see him again. It's not like I go seeking him out.'

Talfrin stood.

'I have one thing,' Rafi said. 'Go to the library, speak to Kazir. He's an old friend of mine. Knows a lot about the city's history, and the Fox's family. He's been avoiding me.'

'You suspect him?'

Rafi shrugged. 'I've spent a lot of time with guilt. My own and others. Recently, Kazir is riddled with it.'

Talfrin thanked the thief and went to leave. As he placed his hand on the door, though, he stopped. The thief watched him with wary eyes, glancing at the Bladekin's sword.

When Talfrin moved, Rafi flinched half a mile. But Talfrin's hand floated past his sword hilt, dipping into his pack.

He pulled out the bag of coins he'd taken from the Mossland bandits and tossed it to Rafi.

'For your rent.'

***

Snow dusted the stone walls and blue slate tiles of the library as it came into view.

'So, this Kazir. What do we know about him?' Nadina asked.

Talfrin rolled the cold out of his shoulders. He still limped slightly from the injury she'd given him. 'Not much beyond his friendship with the thief, and his apparently strange behaviour.'

'Not much of a lead.'

'I trust him.'

She tilted her head. 'You don't seem like someone who trusts easily.'

'I'm not.'

'But you'd trust a thief.'

'Thieves rarely lie,' he said, 'when they have little to lose.'

He pushed the weighty oaken door open and wiped his feet. The roof was tall, the windows long and thin and stretching the entire length of the hall. Beneath them, a few people ambled slowly between the heavy shelves, while others sat at desks and scratched away with pens. The air was heavy with silence and the smell of damp and old paper.

He expected more.

A clerk beckoned them over to a dense desk. She blinked at them, eyes dancing from one to the other.

'This is the library,' she said.

'I know,' Talfrin said.

She cleared her throat. 'Do you have a pass?'

'I do not.'

She flicked her fingers on the desk. 'I can't let you in without permission, I'm sorry.'

'Not even to speak to someone?'

'Who is it you want to speak to?'

'His name's Kazir.'

She paused for a moment, scanning a sheet of paper. Her eyes had dark bags under them, and her robe was creased all over.

He spied Kazir's name amongst the others on the paper. Check-in time, 8am. The other space was blank.

She looked up again. Fingers flicking the desk. She practically radiated anxious energy. Something was up. 'Does he know you're coming?'

No was the obvious answer, but she would turn him away. So he hedged. 'He might. I'm doing some research. A friend told me he might be able to help.'

She smiled a little, a weary smile. 'Research? You don't look the type.'

'Appearances can be deceiving.'

'I didn't mean it like that! It's a good thing! I wish more people like–' she caught herself. 'I wish everyone would engage with the library more. What are you researching?'

'Family history.'

'Your family are from Thrynn?'

He nodded.

'Kazir should be in. Wait here.'

She disappeared behind the shelves.

'Is your family from Thrynn?' Nadina whispered.

He shrugged. 'Could be.'

'You're a stone cold liar,' she said with a smile.

It wasn't something he'd noticed. Wandering from place to place, he'd grown used to inventing stories about himself. Anything he needed to slip by more smoothly.

He didn't respond.

***

The door to Kazir's office was already open.

He was sitting behind his desk, signing papers by the light of a candle. A man with a round head and thin grey hair, his lips were tightly pursed, his eyes heavy.

'Come in,' he said. His voice was deep, but hoarse and dry. 'You are the researchers.'

'That's right,' Talfrin said.

He folded the paper in front of him and stood, pacing across the room. 'Come to look up your family history. That is something I do, as part of my commission to the city.'

'Not my family history, sir. That of another.'

He arched an eyebrow. 'Oh? Do they know about it?'

'I doubt it. They're dead.'

He stopped. 'Ah. We're going to need a different archive for that. This way.' He swept past them. They followed him down a flight of stairs and through a musty corridor. He snatched up a lantern as they went and lit it.

'It's always nice to see new people taking an interest in the archive,' he said, his voice echoing. 'Once you start, you'll have trouble stopping.'

'I don't doubt it,' Talfrin said. Nadina suppressed a snigger.

They entered a room full of shelves, stacked from floor to ceiling in rows. A ladder stood propped against the wall.

'The room where the magic happens,' Kazir said with a smile. 'Now, what was the name?'

'Lovican. Lord Lovican. Otherwise known as the Fox.'

His grin fell away. His cheeks wobbled.

'Lovican.'

'Yes.'

He turned away. 'We have no records of that name here.'

'But you know it.'

'Oh, I know it,' Kazir said. 'He and his family were lords of our city. As such, their records aren't kept here. They were in the castle. And I'm sure you know what happened to that. So I have nothing for you.'

He moved towards the door, but Nadina stood in front of it. She pushed back her cloak, revealing the moonblade.

'You have no personal knowledge of Lovican?' Talfrin continued.

Kazir was trembling. His cheeks burned bright red. 'What do you think you're doing here?'

'I just want some information.'

'I've told you all I'm willing to say,' Kazir said, spreading his arms. 'You're trying to pin the blame for the fires on me. I'm telling you, it has nothing to do with me.'

'Oh no, we know who's setting the fires. We want to know how we can find the Fox.'

Kazir's eyes shined with rage. 'Let me out.'

For a long moment, the scholar's heavy breathing was the only sound in the room. Talfrin's eyes met Nadina's. He gave her a gentle nod and she moved aside, leaving Kazir to scramble down the corridor.

'That went well,' she said with a scowl. 'He doesn't know anything.'

'He knows more than he's letting on,' Talfrin said. 'I think we need a thief.'

***

Rafi eyed up the old library as he'd done so many times before.

The snow and ice would make the roofs perilous. But it was nothing he couldn't handle.

He climbed up the old cart, creeping silently over the tiles, heading towards the window of his friend's office.

As he expected, there was a light inside.

'Kazir,' he whispered. 'What have you got yourself into?'

He held nothing against him. He knew personally how capable the Fox was of twisting people's arms. Sometimes, he broke bones.

Fear seized him, but he calmed himself.

He had a job to do.

Pausing before the final leap, he took a moment to survey the city below. Many chimneys were gently puffing smoke, marring the clear night sky. The occasional window still shone, but most were dark, and the streets were empty. People waiting, cowed by fear, fear he'd helped to sow.

Leaping the gap, he found the ledge was icier than he expected, and his feet nearly slipped from under him. All he could do was cling to a stone lip and peer into the dark below until he regained his balance.

Slowly, inch by inch, he crept over to his friend's office window, through which some excess smoke from the fire was pouring. Kazir always complained his chimney didn't work right. Hours of sitting in a smoky room with his friend had made Rafi curse its existence, but now he offered a prayer of thanks to the Four. That window was his only way in.

He perched by the edge of the frost-coated glass, peering into the room.

The top of his friend's head bobbed below him where he sat at his desk. He was speaking to someone across the room.

A robed and hooded figure concealed in a shadowy corner, fingers steepled.

The Fox. Lord Lovican.

Rafi shook his head. He'd suspected, of course. But what would drive a renowned scholar like Kazir into the arms of the Fox? In Rafi's case, it was the simple promise of coin. But someone on the lord's commission made more than enough to live comfortably.

It was a great gamble on Kazir's part. If Lord Bedivar caught so much as a whiff of suspicion, Kazir would be out on the street.

Could it be that Kazir wasn't being coerced? That he actually wanted Lovican to return?

He couldn't. Rafi remembered when he first came here to ask about Lovican, when he found the pendant. Kazir denounced the man.

Something else was afoot.

He strained, but couldn't make out what they were saying. A crow flew behind him, cawing, causing both men to look up. Rafi ducked out of view.

Had they seen him?

There was a break in their conversation. He held his breath, his heart pounding in his ears. They began to speak again.

When he peeked back, they were deep in conversation.

He caught odd words. A lot of talk about the library. Lord Bedivar was mentioned. Whatever this was, it was important.

One phrase, he heard as clear as day: 'fire wraith.'

He'd heard of fire wraiths, but never seen one in person. He and Talfrin had discussed them for a short while. The Bladekin had supposedly saved one some months ago. But considering Lovican's plans, the implication was clear.

The snap of a book startled him. He looked down to see Kazir on his feet, putting a large, scarlet-bound book back on a shelf in the far corner, leaving a scattering of letters on his desk. At the Fox's beckoning, they left the room.

Rafi seized the opportunity.

Prying the window open a little wider, he dropped onto the shelf below, following years of practise. He jumped down, absorbing the impact with a silent roll, and made his way over to the shelf.

It was a heavy book, the leather spine dry and cracked and the pages crisp. A corner flaked off as he opened it.

The title read: *A Sociological Study of the Fire Wraith.*

A voice echoed from the corridor. The sound of heavy boots, growing louder.

In a panic, Rafi launched himself at the desk, sweeping up the papers scattered there in his arms and scrambling up a bookshelf, perching on top in a shadowed corner of the room.

The door creaked open and Kazir entered. He closed it behind him and leant against it. In the darkening light of evening, his face was lit up gaunt and blue by the glow of a nearby moongem, sitting in a glass container and pulsing slowly.

After a moment of silence, Kazir made his way to his desk.

He froze when he saw the missing papers.

'Rafi,' he uttered, so quietly the thief barely heard him.

'Rafi!' he shouted.

The thief flinched.

'Come out. We need to talk.'

Rafi didn't move.

'I promise I can explain.'

The thief's hand slid to his belt, where the dagger was safely back in its sheath. He hopped down.

Kazir's face was haggard and forlorn, but he smiled. 'I should've known better than to try to sneak something past you.'

Rafi said nothing, but kept his eyes on his old friend. Any sudden movement, he'd strike. He'd deal with the consequences after.

'You aren't going to need that blade,' he said.

'You said you could explain,' Rafi said, drawing the dagger and twirling it through his fingers. 'Go ahead.'

Kazir's smile evaporated. 'Last I heard, you were working for the Fox, too.' He grinned at Rafi's shock. 'He told me.'

'Not anymore.'

'No? A sudden strike of morality, after all this time?'

'He's a dangerous man, Kazir.'

'And yet you did his bidding. You terrorised the people of this city. You passed his trinket on instead of destroying it. You set his fires.'

'I did what I had to do to survive,' Rafi said.

Kazir's face darkened. He paced slowly. 'Don't we all.'

'I had no choice. I was an inch away from living on the streets. An inch from death.'

'You think I wasn't forced, too?'

'How could you be?' Rafi said. 'You have money. No family. Plenty to eat. How could he possibly threaten you?'

'Tell me, Rafi. What happens when books meet fire?'

A ghost of a vision filled his mind, of the library with flames licking from the windows, crowds gathering to watch as scholars burst from the doors, their robes alight.

He shook his head. Could the pendant be in his mind still, after all this time?

'He wants to burn the library.'

'He wants to burn down the whole damn city,' Kazir said and slammed his fist on the desk. When he looked up, there were tears on his cheeks. 'You think I wanted this? He wants to purge the city. To make it anew. Only a madman could want that.'

'So why did he need you?'

'Only one creature has the power to do such a thing.'

He remembered the book. 'The fire wraiths.'

'Yes. So I bargained with him. I would help him meet them. They would follow through with it; they hate the cities. I would show him how to find them, and in return… he would spare the library. It would be the beacon of his new city. He would bring me moongems and fund any such research as we deemed necessary.'

'You'd sacrifice the city for the sake of a few books?'

Kazir turned away, casting his gaze over the shelves. 'You were a student of books once, Rafi.'

'Human lives are more important.'

'He's going to burn the city regardless,' he snapped. 'There's no stopping that. But if I can preserve their words, their knowledge… then at least a ghost of Thrynn will endure.'

'What if there was a way to stop him?'

Kazir shook his head. 'You're a fool, Rafi. You don't know his power.'

'There is a way. We have a Bladekin.'

The old scholar looked up, eyes shining in the blue light. For the first time, it seemed they held a glimmer of hope. 'A Bladekin? They don't meddle in affairs like this. Besides, they'd need a powerful weapon to confront a foe like him.'

'This one has come to destroy the pendant. His friend wields a moonblade.'

'His friend? They are a Bladekin, too?'

'No.'

'So they can intervene without breaking the code.' A smile spread across Kazir's face. 'A moonblade. That might do it.'

***

Talfrin woke drenched in sweat. His hand scrabbled to his chest, clutching the pendant tight.

'Another bad dream?' Nadina asked. She was standing at the foot of his bed, already suited up in her armour. Sunlight streamed through the window.

She'd been able to fulfil his request: they had separate beds. Just in the same room.

He grunted as he sat up. 'It's nothing.'

'What did he show you this time?'

The Bladekin was silent, letting himself properly awaken. The dream was already slipping from his memory, but the emotions – the anger, the pride – sat heavy in his chest.

'A new city,' he said. 'I had power.'

'Do you think it was meant as a message?'

The question irritated him, but he didn't know why. 'I don't know. We don't know how this magic works. It might not even be conscious.'

She tilted her head. There was a strange look in her eyes that he couldn't place. 'You need to destroy it.'

'I know,' he said sharply. He averted his eyes, aware that he was being irrational. 'I'm going to the baths,' he said.

'Good idea.'

He joined the other morning bathers in the hot water, sinking into the steaming liquid and forcing all thoughts from his head. He focused on the chatter, the soft strumming of the musician's lute, and felt the knots loosen in his shoulders. *Relax. Breathe. Calm.*

She was right. He had to destroy it.

But there was a deep sadness in him at that thought. Though they'd only been with him a short time, he would dearly miss the dreams. He couldn't even say why. They felt familiar.

He could already sense a change in himself. He felt stronger, more certain. The self-doubt and worry was dripping away, bit by bit.

It was a hard thing to give away.

He stood, taking one of the free towels and walking back to the changing rooms. The cold air nipped his skin. When he found a cubicle, he sat, and stayed there. He didn't move until he was bone dry.

On his way back into the street, he ran into Rafi, who, for the first time, had a big smile on his face.

'I've been looking all over for you,' he said. 'Where've you been?'

'Bathing.'

'I'm surprised you don't look like a prune.'

Insolent. The thief was clearly in a good mood. 'Were you successful?'

'Very much so. Lovican plans to use some fire wraiths to burn the city down.'

Talfrin grimaced. 'And that's good news?'

'No. The good news is that we know where to find them.'

Rafi described a clearing further down the west road, deep within the Woldland woods.

'You expect me to fight a host of fire wraiths?'

'No, I expect you to *talk* to a host of fire wraiths. You've done it before, right?'

Fire wraiths were difficult beings to speak with at the best of times, even in the wilds of the Mosslands. Those who lived here in the Woldland, where hunters and poachers lurked around every corner and nature had been reduced to little more than a curiosity, would be savage creatures indeed.

'These will be different.'

Rafi frowned. He seemed to be weighing his words. When he spoke again, it was slow and deliberate. 'I owe the people of Thrynn for what I did to them. What I've done to them my whole life. I will go with you. Between the three of us, surely we must stand some kind of chance?'

Rafi was right. With the three of them, especially Nadina's moonblade, there was some slim chance of walking out alive.

Besides, he'd come this far. It was time to see this through to its conclusion.

'I'm never getting involved in politics again,' Talfrin muttered.

'What?'

'Nothing. Let's go find Nadina.'

***

The forests of the Woldland felt like home to Talfrin. Autumnal smells of fresh rain and rotting leaves lifted his spirits, and he absorbed the beautiful silvery shine of the birch trees and the golden leaves that sheeted the old road. Focusing on the sound of Spens's hooves crunching through the fallen leaves, he took a deep breath. Though much of Guenteria was warmer than he liked, the Woldlands were more temperate. The scholars said it was something to do with the sea and the currents.

It was a great distraction.

They walked in silence, Rafi and Nadina either side of him, both on foot. Rafi's eyes remained on the ground. Nadina looked everywhere other than at him.

The air was heavy.

'Much further?' Talfrin asked.

'Not much,' Rafi said. His hand hovered over his dagger subconsciously. 'A little way now.'

'Don't flash your blade around them,' Talfrin said. 'Unless you want to be turned into beef.'

'Any other advice?' Rafi asked, lips tight.

He felt the rage in his stomach. 'Just say nothing. Let me talk.'

Rafi looked away.

'Neither of us have ever seen one,' Nadina said. 'You can't blame him for being curious.'

Talfrin took in the words in silence. She was right. The rational part of his mind recognised it.

The emotions were more powerful than ever.

He was torn between a desire to toss the pendant into the undergrowth and to clutch it tighter and never let go.

'They don't like us,' he said after a while. 'If they had their way, they'd wipe the entire world of humanity. They aren't known for their reason and kindness.'

'So how do we convince them to turn against Lovican?'

'You let me worry about that.'

'That's hard to do when my life depends on it,' Rafi said.

Talfrin smiled, and patted the green bottle at his belt, the one the witch gave him. He hoped and prayed it would be enough.

The day changed as they climbed the last hill. Mist descended, obscuring the valley. The branches of naked trees stretched out, clawing at his cloak with knobbly fingers as the forest grew thicker.

It wasn't long past midday, but the sky was darkening as though it were already dusk. A stiff wind shook the branches and sent leaves skittering down the slope.

'Should be somewhere around here,' Rafi whispered.

'What are we looking for?'

'Stones of some sort. Standing stones.'

'An altar of some kind?' Nadina asked.

Talfrin scanned the lumpy highland.

'Perhaps once,' Rafi said. 'I don't know. That's what Kazir told me.'

'There,' Talfrin said, pointing.

He'd seen them before, though rarely. Three stacks of rocks piled up to head height, a triangular boulder sitting on top. Three perfectly smooth sides forming a sharp point, like three fingers holding an arrowhead, aiming at the heavens.

Beside it was a large brazier carved from stone, cradling a fire that flickered lazily, unaffected by the wind. The flames moved softly like dancers at a ball, robed in yellow and orange gowns. To anyone else's eye, they would have looked entirely ordinary.

But he knew different.

'*Kneel*,' a wispy voice said.

'Do as they say,' Talfrin said, dropping to one knee and keeping his eyes on the ground. The others did the same.

'*Intruders.*'

'Not intruders,' he said. 'We wish to speak with you. Then we'll leave.'

'*Come for our land*,' a sharper voice said.

'*They've taken enough.*'

'*Come for more.*'

'*Must fight.*'

He looked up to see three flames gliding across the ground, evaporating the moisture below them and leaving a trail of steam as they approached. Each had two flameless gaps which served as eyes, and they all glared at him.

'No,' he said, climbing to his feet. 'You have my word. We wish to speak with you. About Lovican.'

'*Lovican?*'

'The Grey Man.'

'*Grey Man. Where is he?*'

'He's not with us. He's a foe of ours.'

The air crackled. Two of the fire wraiths grew in size. The surrounding mist steamed.

'*Enemy!*'

They came forward. But the one wraith which hadn't grown or spoken stayed still, and uttered one word.

'*Bladekin.*'

Talfrin looked right into its eyes, and he recognised it.

'*Bladekin.*'

'I know you,' he said.

'*Bladekin.*'

'You're a long way from the Mosslands.'

The other two stopped, shrinking back to their original size. The one he knew turned to white flame.

'*Known?*'

'*Known. We hear him.*'

They retreated, hovering in a line in front of the stones. The white one drifted forward.

'*Speak.*'

'You won't like my words.'

'*Return the favour.*'

'I'll be blunt. You need to break with Lovican.'

They flared, the flames skirting his face. Rafi stumbled backwards, drawing their attention. One started stalking him, watching like a wolf, but Talfrin stepped between them.

'*Betrayal.*'

'I speak the truth. You'll gain nothing from working with him.'

'*Land.*'

'*Burn.*'

'*Restore.*'

'Is that what he promised you? He promised you the land?'

'*Grey Man is their foe. Our friend.*'

'He's playing you for fools,' Talfrin said, knowing that would get a response. 'He is their foe. But he's not your friend. He wants that land for himself. To build a new city.'

There was a hiss of anger and the air filled with smoke. A nearby tree burst into flame as though struck by lightning.

'*Lies. Lies.*'

'*Humans all lie.*'

The white wraith stayed silent.

'You may not want to hear it, but it's the truth. He used my friend here, and his friend too. He has a silver tongue. But those words are just smoke. There's no fire in him.'

'*Liar!*'

The white wraith drifted closer, its eyes on him. '*You lie for yourself.*'

'You can trust me. I tell the truth.'

'*Grey Man is selfish. So are you. So are all people.*'

'I have no selfishness in me.'

The wraiths circled him – slowly at first, then faster and faster. They stirred the leaves up in their wake, and some caught fire before being spat out to lie smoking on the earth. A thin laughter filled the air.

'*No selfishness.*'

'*All men are selfish.*'

'You may find that city distasteful,' he said defiantly. 'But people live there. They didn't build it. They were just born there, they know nothing else. You can't hold them accountable for their ancestors' sins.'

The circling slowed.

'*Just as selfish.*'

'*Liar.*'

'I am not lying to you.'

The white wraith was hovering in front of him again.

'*Grey Man lies. You lie.*'

He said nothing, but held its gaze as it stared him down. It grew until it loomed over him and he felt the heat on his face.

'*Proof.*'

'Proof?'

'*Prove your selflessness. Destroy it.*'

He knew what it meant.

The coals of rage burned in his stomach. *No,* a voice inside him said. *No. It's yours.*

He raised his hand and his fingers were trembling.

Reaching up, he grasped the pendant around his neck.

And his head snapped backwards.

He was in another part of the forest, soaring forward with great speed. A pit of anger in his stomach which could have burned to the core of the earth. Long, grey fingers stretched out in front of him, not his own. Snaking up his forearm were arcane tattoos which even he didn't recognise, swirling patterns entwined with ancient runes.

Talfrin felt very real fear. His own fear.

Don't do it, the voice said. *Stay still.*

For a single, lucid moment, he was aware his body was shaking, the white wraith still hovering implacably before him. Nadina gripped his arm, her fingers cold.

Lovican yanked him back.

A wave of calm. Confidence. He was relaxing in a huge, bright bathhouse with marble walls and beautiful blue water. Servants stood to attention, waiting for him. One clutched a handful of his old clothes; the other held bright, vibrant threads he'd only seen worn by nobles, neatly folded and waiting.

The other held a crown. A Durmedian crown.

He knew it was his.

Outside the windows, flames licked the night sky and hands clawed at the glass.

A cry tore him back to reality.

The wraiths scattered as Lovican burst into the clearing. He pounced on Rafi before Talfrin could move, angling a blade at his throat.

Nadina was nowhere to be seen.

'You can't harm me,' Lovican said. His voice came from deep in his throat, sounding at once young and unfathomably old. 'Do not move, Talfrin. Leave that pendant where it is.'

Talfrin stayed still.

He wasn't sure what he'd expected from the ancient tyrant of Thrynn. He wore a deep red doublet and black breeches, both of which might once have been grand, but were now threadbare. His long, white hair formed a widow's peak, though it had fallen away in clumps. His grey skin was stretched thinly over his skull.

Rafi was panting heavily, eyes wide, hands clutching his attacker's arm, which was wrapped around his throat.

Talfrin noticed the snaking tattoos and ancient runes woven in.

'You've fallen so far, Keeper.'

Lovican's eyes landed on his. Talfrin's head was filled with memories not his own. *He saw the standing stones. A pyramid-shaped candle burned before them, surrounded by twelve perfect flowers.*

'You know nothing of me,' Lovican said.

'I know enough of your kind.'

A weary smile spread across Lovican's face. 'There aren't many of us now.'

'You still have a task to do. A task you failed.'

'Don't lecture me, Bladekin. You do more harm to this world than I have ever done. All that great work, destroyed at your hand.'

'For the safety of humanity.'

'It will lead to their ruin.' He smiled. 'Now, give me that pendant.'

Give me that pendant.

Talfrin grimaced. 'No.'

Lovican angled his blade at Rafi's throat. The ancient lord arched an eyebrow. 'You want his blood on your hands, too?'

'If it saves the city.'

Rafi's eyes widened.

Lovican scoffed. 'So much for the defender of humanity. I'm a Keeper. Your blade won't harm me. I'll kill him, kill you, and the city will burn. Wraiths or not. You could, at least, spare his life.'

Talfrin eyed up the white wraith, which hovered silently ten feet away.

Don't do it. Give it to me.

Nadina was still missing.

But he knew where she was. He glanced up, seeing her disguised amongst the branches of the tree. The assassin, waiting for her moment to strike.

'*Do it.*'

His fingers wouldn't. He couldn't destroy it. *It's too precious. Too important. Give it to me!*

He pulled the bottle from his belt and drank.

***

Talfrin was kneeling in the middle of a misty clearing, though he couldn't remember why.

To his right, three fire wraiths lingered, one as white as the moon. His whole body trembled, though he couldn't remember why.

An elderly Keeper stood to his left, clutching a ragged young man in his arms, angling a blade at his throat. Talfrin cared about the thief, though he couldn't remember why.

The Keeper stared intently.

'Give it to me,' he said.

Talfrin looked at the piece of jewellery around his neck. He cupped it in his hands. It was hot to the touch, scorching him through his gloves. It was fashioned to look like a fox – a beautiful, silver fox, with orange gemstone eyes that seemed to plead with him.

He'd once felt some powerful connection to it, but he couldn't remember why.

The Keeper was shaking, and Talfrin felt some strong energy from him. As though a battering ram were slamming against the gate of his mind. For now, it held firm.

By his knees was a green bottle, a thin, dark liquid spilling from it onto the damp, saturated earth and soaking into his breeches.

There was something he did remember.

The Moonblade Princess was missing. But he knew where she was.

And he knew his purpose again.

He tore the pendant from his neck, rolling as he did. The Keeper screamed. The white wraith shone impossibly bright, blinding them all. Talfrin tossed the pendant towards it.

He pulled his shield from his back and crouched behind it as flames flew past him.

A pain clutched his body, as though he'd been engulfed in fire. It made him unable to think, unable to see.

His soul screamed as the wraith ate the cursed, twisted pendant.

He fell.

***

When he regained consciousness, a deep coldness was seeping into his skin.

He was lying on the ground. Raindrops tickled his face. There was no sound beyond the whistle of the wind through the branches.

Glancing around, he saw Nadina, whose face was red and puffy. Her eyes shone; tears glistened on her cheeks.

Lord Lovican lay at her feet, face in the mud.

The lunar-white blade in her hand was dripping red.

***

That night, it snowed in Thrynn.

Talfrin rested in his bed under a latticed window, focusing on the crackling of the dying fire in the corner of the room. Heat was easing the tightness in his muscles, but he knew the dull ache would still be there for a few days.

On the other side of the room, Nadina slept. It hadn't taken her long to slip off once they got back. Her mouth was open slightly, her face relaxed. She looked peaceful.

He felt more at peace than he had in weeks. His mind was his own again. In the midst of it, he hadn't noticed how deep Lovican's thoughts had merged with his own.

In the hours since, his memories had slowly knitted themselves back together, though patches remained. He was sure they would fill in, given time. There was no doubt in his mind the witch had given him a memory potion. Without it, he wasn't sure he'd have had the strength.

Despite the newfound silence, there were worries that plagued him.

Lovican was a Keeper. Keepers never behaved that way. It was their first rule: Interfere not in the affairs of the present.

What had possessed him? And could others follow the same path?

What would have happened to Thrynn if he hadn't intervened?

And though he was gone, an echo of Lovican's memory remained.

Talfrin feared what he'd see when he slept.

Sitting up, he took a deep breath and collected himself. It was no use lying here, wallowing.

He needed some fresh air.

A veil of snow had settled on the roofs and streets of Thrynn. He shrugged deeper into his blue-and-white-checked cloak and leant against the wall of the inn. The city was deserted, all lights were out beside the odd flickering candle in an upstairs window where the night folks sat up reading or fretting. There was still an air of anxiety in the city, but he smiled. That would lift soon. There would be no more fires, no more complaints of fiery apparitions in the dark.

Life would return to normal.

He'd saved some lives, destroyed a dangerous magical object, and restored order. In the end, it was Nadina who struck the fatal blow.

The Bladekin code was safe.

But this time he was determined: no more politics. It was time to find something easier. A tutorship, far away from the dangers of the world.

Some peace at last.

Sudden movement caught his eye in an alleyway further down the street. He watched.

Again.

'Rafi,' he said.

The thief stepped out of the shadows. 'I must be losing my touch,' he said. 'Second time I've been caught in as many days.'

'You never were a natural thief. You belong behind a book somewhere.'

Rafi smiled. 'That's why I'm here, actually.' He unclipped his sheath and dagger from his belt, holding them out. 'I wanted you to have this.'

Talfrin shook his head. 'You're a fool, Rafi. If you don't want it, sell it. You need the money.'

'I need it much less now, thanks to you,' he said, patting the pouch at his side. 'And I wanted to… to make it up to you. For reminding me who I am and dragging me out of that situation.'

Talfrin shuffled. 'You don't owe me anything.'

There was a brief silence between them. 'What will you do now?' Rafi asked.

'I'm looking at a career in education.'

Rafi laughed. 'No, I'm being serious. Back to Durm, perhaps?'

'I'm serious. No adventuring for me for a while. Though I have to get that moonblade from Nadina. Friend or not, I'm duty-bound to destroy it.'

Cold fingers settled on his neck, and a white blade appeared before his throat.

'Good luck with that,' Nadina whispered in his ear, making him flinch.

He pushed away, turning to face her. 'I thought you were asleep.'

'I was, until you blundered out. You make more noise than a giant.'

Rafi sniggered.

Talfrin shot him a look. 'Keep those thoughts to yourself.'

She levelled him with those calculating green eyes, the same eyes as the king of Voleren. Eyes which saw right through him.

'I heard you say you're thinking of quitting.'

'Not quitting. Pivoting.'

Her dark lips split into a smile. 'That won't happen. You were made to walk the shield road.'

EPILOGUE

Talfrin walked the shield road, and he was cold. His feet were aching and frigid. The sole of his left boot had cracked. They were new, too – or at least, they still felt it. *Especially for warriors*, the seller had told him. *Your feet will never tire*. He could have laughed, but in that short time, he'd walked the breadth of the world, from the Mosslands in the east to Volur City on the western coast, and from there to Thrynn in the far south, in lush Guenteria.

The temptation to return home, to the land of Tovenar where he was born, was strong.

But Nadina was right. That wasn't the life for him.

He smiled, despite his cracked boot and the chill in the air which made his muscles ache and his sleep restless. Because when he was here, leading Spens by the reins, his sword belt rattle the only sound in his ears, he felt whole.

Nadina walked ahead, her dark cloak swishing just above the mud, glancing around at the thin woodland they walked through. His foot still ached from her attack, but he didn't hold it against her. If anything, it was a comfort to know he was travelling with someone who could match his skills.

The hills were gentle, and occasionally they saw a deer or two watching them from afar, munching on whatever foliage they could still find. He watched, thinking back on their last day in the Woldlands.

His memory of the confrontation with Lovican was still patchy, and he was beginning to accept that he'd never fully grasp what had happened. But that didn't bother him much. The outcome had been the best he could have hoped for, all told.

Now they would face the aftermath.

He did not want to be in the room when the Bladekin scholars at Kadahrn and the Keepers finally met. Perhaps the Gilgaran king would have to mediate.

He took a deep breath, focusing on the road ahead, the rhythmic fall of his feet on the earth and the smell of musty, rotting leaves. That wasn't his problem to deal with.

He'd done his part.

***

They came across a ruin on the left side of the road as the sun set. It was a low, circular building, surrounded by erratic stones and covered in moss, so much that it blended in with the trees and grass. He would have missed it entirely if he hadn't seen the flicker of a fire through one of the large, empty windows.

They approached slowly. The ruin itself had no floor beyond bare earth. In the centre was a makeshift firepit surrounded by two bedrolls, some sacks and a peculiarly-shaped red bottle. A horse was bound to a standing stone. It shuffled, the whites of its eyes showing.

A shout came from not far away.

'That sounded like someone calling for help,' Nadina said.

Talfrin didn't move.

She glowered. 'Come on!'

'It's not our business.'

She set off without another word. With an exasperated sigh, he followed her, leaving Spens in the ruin.

She was too brave. Too ready to be a hero.

But he quite liked that.

They raced deeper into the woods, leaping fallen branches and hidden ditches carrying tiny streams. They came to a clearing where a warrior stood holding a torch high against the encroaching night, sending the shadows of the surrounding trees flickering. Her dark hair was tied up tight on top of her head. Her armour clinked as she paced from side to side like a caged wolf, her axe at the ready.

'Leave him, you vile creatures!'

As they burst into the clearing the woman spun around, eyes wild, nearly slicing Talfrin in two. He parried.

'We're here to help you!'

Her eyes were dark and full of suspicion, her skin the rough, ragged texture of someone who'd seen a lot of the road. A look Talfrin had seen all too often.

'You have moon essence?'

Talfrin produced a small phial of rainbow-coloured oil. As he did, a shattering scream made them all cover their ears.

'Shadow wraiths,' Talfrin said, and oiled his blade with the corner of his cloak. He did the same for the warrior, who lurched forward without another word.

Talfrin and Nadina followed her.

They found a young man curled up at the base of a tree, clutching a dim torch in both hands. His blade lay shattered on the ground, and his shoulders had the judder of hypothermia. His hands shook so much, he could barely grip the light.

Half a dozen shadows circled him, their maws gaping as they sucked the warmth from the air, leaving him to freeze. Their sharp eyes locked on the newcomers.

Talfrin seized the initiative, sweeping forward with a quick uppercut and cleaving one in two. The others swirled like startled bats, flitting around him. He felt a numbing touch grasp his abdomen, making him flinch away.

The warrior was grunting like she was possessed, swinging torch and axe alike in savage arcs, hoping to catch one of them. A curdling wail filled the sky as she sliced one in half; it fell to the earth in two sharp, shadowy ribbons.

Nadina, swift and deadly, pierced one right through the heart. The moonblade glowed and the wraith screamed and shrank and vanished.

The others disappeared into the gathering night, screeching.

The woman ran straight to the young man's side. In the light, Talfrin saw his face: clean skin, a light beard and black hair that was in the awkward stage between a neat cut and fully grown out. His clothing was of an excellent quality, made with rich dyes, but it was caked in mud now.

'Theod, are you okay?' she asked.

'I'm fine,' he said through chattering teeth, as the warrior threw a cloak around him. Talfrin was reminded of a lioness trying to protect a cub.

Together, they made their way back to the ruin where Spens was waiting patiently beside the other horse.

'Seems like Boc has taken a liking to your beast,' the warrior said. 'Strange, he's usually wary of others.' She extended her hand. 'I'm Rensa. Thank you for helping me.'

The words were crisp and wooden, the handshake overly formal, but Talfrin accepted them anyway. They seemed sincere.

They settled around the fire. Talfrin eased his boots off, basking in the relief, and chewed on some beef jerky. As much as he enjoyed his solitary journeys, having the company lifted his mood.

Their new companions were cuddled close together by the fire, Rensa watching Theod's every move. He shrugged her off with a reassuring pat, grabbing some hard bread from one of their sacks.

'So where are you headed?' Talfrin asked.

'South,' Rensa said. 'Looking for work.'

'Apparently this is what I do now,' Theod said with a little smile.

'Mercenaries?' Talfrin asked.

'Swords for hire. We're a team.'

'Are you… wed?' Talfrin asked.

'Of course not,' Rensa said quickly.

'I was just curious, since he's Guenterian.'

'We haven't known each other very long,' Theod said, his cheeks blushing slightly.

'Only a few months,' Rensa confirmed, 'but we're already close. Our bond was forged in ice and iron.'

'She's being dramatic,' Theod said. 'We bonded while working for a witch. White-haired, she was, with a scar at the right corner of her mouth. Knew both of us were coming. She seemed to know we'd get together from the very start, in fact.'

Talfrin paused at those words. They were too familiar.

He glanced at Nadina. She was watching him with those familiar green eyes, the eyes which seemed to see right to his heart.

He wondered if it was the same witch. And if the same games were at play here.

But even if they were, he didn't care. The past was behind him.

And there was no-one else he'd rather walk beside as he travelled the shield road.

ACKNOWLEDGEMENTS

Writing a book is never a lone endeavour, and many hands have helped carry this one over the line. I would like to say thank you to my beta readers and critiquers for helping to whip these words into shape, and to Lou, Ashley, Thomas, Sean, Jessika, Em, Xenia, Viv, Sammi and Jaecyn in particular for lending me their thoughts and their editorial expertise. Without them, this collection would have been much weaker.

Beyond that, I'm incredibly grateful for my writing friends, who have given me constant encouragement and companionship as we walk this particular shield road together. It has been a joy to get to know you all, albeit at a great (social) distance.

I would like to thank my family, for being nothing but encouraging of my dreams from the start; you allowed the flame to spark. I would like to thank my high school teachers for providing the kindling, and my creative writing tutors at Keele University, who fanned the flames. And, lastly, a thank you to my uni friends, who will remain friends for life no matter what.

It goes without saying that any mistakes remaining in the text are my fault alone – I've read it enough times!

THE AUTHOR

Dewi is a fantasy author who spends much of his time writing outside, wiping raindrops off his laptop screen. His flash fiction piece 'Maccabeus' won second place in Grindstone Literary's 'Open Prose Competition 2017', and his short story 'Swamplights' appears in *Chimera*, an anthology published by Lost Boys Press.

He's also an illustrator, having worked with over 40 authors to create maps for their books – of settings both real and fictional.

He lurks on Twitter almost constantly: you can find him at @Dewiwrites.

(For more information, head to dewihargreaves.com)

Printed in Great Britain
by Amazon